# DON'T FEED THE TROLL!

Praise for
John Hickman's

# FREAKS UNITED

Shortlisted for the
*James Reckitt Hull Children's Book Award*

'It's a real romp and I was laughing throughout.'
*Jake Hope, Costa Children's Book Award judge
and Chair of the CILIP Youth Libraries Group*

'John Hickman makes heroes of the loners
and the less gifted, showing that football is about
more than just being the best; it's about enjoying
yourself and playing as a team. If you don't know
your left foot from your right – and even if you
do – *Freaks United* is a book you'll love. It's great!'
*Bali Rai, author and Reading Ahead Ambassador
for the Reading Agency*

JOHN HICKMAN

DON'T FEED THE TROLL!

award

ISBN 978-1-78270-322-8

Cover artwork by Patrick Knowles
Pattern illustrations: Ohn Mar/Shutterstock.com,
Perfectorius/Shutterstock.com

First published by Award Publications Limited 2019

Published by Award Publications Limited,
The Old Riding School, Welbeck,
Worksop, S80 3LR

19 1

Printed in the United Kingdom

*For Abby, Brooke,*
*Finn and Siobhan*

# CONTENTS

Bubblegum Ice Cream.............................11

A Big Decision ...................................16

A Bold Move.....................................22

Dear Chloe.......................................28

A Love Letter ....................................34

A Massive Mistake...............................37

Troll Boy .........................................42

Followers.........................................48

Action! ...........................................53

Mum and Dad ...................................58

The Fall Out .....................................67

Serious Trouble...................................72

Attack of the Troll-lings.........................77

The Message......................................85

Little Jacky ......................................91

Conjuration ......................................98

A Growing Problem ............................106

Bad to Worse....................................115

Chloe and Isaac.................................124

The Curse of Jack...................................................129
An Unlikely Ally...................................................136
Don't Feed the Troll.............................................141
The Prom............................................................146

# DON'T FEED THE TROLL

# BUBBLEGUM ICE CREAM

'How much do you *lurve* Chloe?' Cora whispered to Jack.

Jack didn't answer. He was too busy staring at the back of Chloe's head.

Cora nudged Jack in the ribs.

'Ow!' said Jack. 'What you doing?'

'I was just saying,' said Cora. 'How much do you *lurve* Chloe?'

Jack blinked. He could feel himself getting hot. He scratched the back of his neck. 'What you asking that for?'

"Cos you've been staring at her for the last five minutes.'

Jack looked around the classroom. Mr Cooper was at the front talking about some book. He had a big smile on his face, so Jack could tell it was a book he really liked. Cora was right. Jack *had* been staring at Chloe. He'd just zoned out of the lesson. It happened sometimes. When he was tired or bored or his brain had been stuffed with too much stuff, he'd just sort of go into stand by mode. He was on, but he needed someone to press a button to get him to work. And usually, when he was in standby mode, his eyes would be drawn to Chloe.

'You so *lurve* her!' said Cora.

Jack nudged Cora this time. He glared at his friend. 'Stop saying "lurve" you loser!' he whispered.

Cora was the same age as Jack. Twelve years and seven months. OK, Cora was a month older. But that was no big deal. It was hard for Jack to get annoyed with Cora. She had one of those faces. A round head, dimples, always smiling. The pair of them had been best friends since junior school.

'I don't love her,' whispered Jack.

'Yeah right,' said Cora.

'What? I don't.'

'You so do.'

'I so don't.'

'You proper do, just admit it.'

'I proper don't.'

'Liar.'

'Loser.'

'Freak.'

'Geek.'

Cora frowned at Jack. Her eye twitched.

'Go on,' said Jack. 'Your turn.'

Cora shook her head. 'I'm all out.'

They both laughed.

'Anything you'd like to share with the rest of us?' asked Mr Cooper from the front of the class.

Everyone in class turned around and looked at Jack and Cora. Jack's heart stopped. He hated it when the attention was on him. It made him hot and nervous. Isaac Strong smirked at Jack. Isaac Strong was always smirking at Jack. It was like he thought he was better than him or something.

Fortunately for Jack, he had a way with words. 'The gift of the gab', his mum called it. He could talk his way out of most situations.

'We were just enjoying the lesson,' said Jack.

Mr Cooper squinted at the pair. 'A likely story,' he said.

'It's true, Sir,' said Jack. 'I could listen to you all day long.'

Mr Cooper squinted a bit more, sort of smiled, then carried on talking about whatever it was he was talking about. Within a couple of minutes, Jack had zoned out all over again. And as usual, his eyes and mind had drifted over to Chloe Jones.

She was sitting couple of tables ahead, to Jack's right, sketching something in her exercise book. She was always sketching and drawing, and she was really good too. She had her artwork up in the corridors around the school. From Jack's very first day at Wolfchester High, Chloe had caught his attention. All the new Year Sevens had gathered in the gym, so Locky, the Headmaster, could welcome them. It was the streak of blue in her hair that did it. It was the colour of a tropical ocean or bubblegum ice cream. Jack figured that anyone who had a streak of blue hair must have something about them. It just screamed, 'Look at me! I've got bright blue in my hair. And you know what? I don't care!' Once he'd got over her hair, Jack noticed other things about Chloe. The dark make-up around her eyes. The stud in her nose. To top it all off, she wore these boots. Big, chunky DMs. Not like the dainty little flat shoes or sneakers the other girls at school wore. Jack imagined she could kick his face in if she felt like it. Some schools probably wouldn't have liked nose studs and bright blue streaks in people's hair, but Wolfchester was pretty relaxed. Not that that would've bothered Chloe. Chloe didn't care what anyone thought about her. She didn't try to fit in. Jack wished he didn't care what people thought about him. He wished he didn't want to fit in. He thought that if he could get to know Chloe and hang out with her, then *maybe* some of her attitude would rub off on him.

There was just one problem: Isaac Strong. Isaac Strong was one of the meanest, most snide kids in the whole school. And he was Chloe's best friend. Isaac was tall and skinny. He had dark hair, which he wore in a side-parting. He wore eyeliner too, and he had this weird earring that made him have a hole in his earlobe. Cora reckoned Isaac could keep his Polos in his ear if he wanted. Plus, he dressed like it was Halloween all year round. He wore dark skinny jeans and a long black coat. The other kids called Chloe and Isaac The Witches of Wolfchester. So, while Jack had made his mind up to get to know Chloe and maybe even one day hang out with her, his plan hadn't gone anywhere because of Isaac.

Isaac in-the-way-all-the-flipping-time Strong.

# A BIG DECISION

At break, once Cora and Jack had fought their way through the crowd of kids and bought some crisps and pop from the tuck shop, they stood in front of the noticeboard. There was a big poster for Year Eights' end of year prom. It was purple with silver writing and lots of stars around its edges.

Jack stared at it sadly.

'What's up?' asked Cora.

'Nothing,' said Jack.

'You don't wanna go, do you?' she asked.

'No way,' Jack lied.

Cora smiled at him – this weird frowny smile.

'What?' asked Jack.

'Nothing.'

The pair headed outside. It was summer, so it was warm and bright. The school field had just been mowed and the smell of freshly cut grass filled the air.

Jack and Cora wandered onto the field, where some Year Tens were having a game of Royal Rumble.

Some of them had put their ties around their heads and they were wrestling and throwing each other around like idiots.

'Look at them,' said Cora. 'Numpties.'

Jack snickered and took a swig from his can of Rocket Cola.

'You coming over to mine tonight?' asked Jack.

Cora nodded. 'Yeah, what's the plan?'

'Dad's getting me the new *Kings of Dread*. Thought we could play that.'

'Cool,' said Cora. Finishing her crisps, she opened the packet wide, tilted her head back and tipped the remaining crumbs into her mouth.

Jack watched as she munched away. 'Nice are they?' he asked.

Cora nodded and made this 'hmm-mm' sound. Then she slapped Jack on the arm and pointed over towards the back of the field.

Jack looked across. Beyond a Year Ten who was banging his chest like King Kong, Chloe and Isaac were sitting on the grass.

Cora mumbled something incomprehensible. Bright orange crisp crumbs and spit sprayed from her mouth.

Jack blinked and wiped of the half-chewed crisps off his cheek. 'You what?' he asked.

She swallowed down her mouthful and tried again.

'You gonna ask Chloe to the prom?'

Jack shook his head.

'But you have to,' said Cora.

'Why?'

'Because you *lurve* her.'

'Would you stop saying that!' snapped Jack.

'Just do it. Just go and ask her.'

'No way,' said Jack. 'I couldn't.'

'Why couldn't you?'

'Just because.'

'That's the lamest answer ever. What's the worst that could happen?'

Jack played out all the scenarios in his head. He imagined getting himself all tongue-tied and flustered. He imagined peeing his pants, right there, right in front of Isaac and Chloe. He imagined himself getting kicked in the face by one of Chloe's boots.

'Lots of things,' said Jack.

'But what if she said yes?'

'She wouldn't.'

'She might,' said Cora.

'I don't think she would. Look at her.'

Cora shielded her eyes from the sun and looked out across the field.

'And look at me,' said Jack.

Cora turned around to Jack. She sort of grinned. 'OK, I see what you're saying.'

Jack sighed.

'But she might actually like you back. Stranger things have happened.'

'Like what?'

'Aliens.'

'When did aliens happen?'

'Ghosts then. Ghosts have happened.'

'Just forget it.'

Jack was about to walk away, when Cora grabbed him. 'She *might* like you. I mean, you're not ugly or anything are you?'

Jack thought about it. He wasn't bad looking, no. But he wasn't good looking either. Not like Omar Croft in Year Ten. Now he *was* good-looking. Jack knew this for certain because 'Omar Croft is fit' had been written, lots of times, all over the place – the toilet walls, in the gym, someone had even written it on the front of one of Jack's exercise books. Omar was definitely handsome. Even Jack knew that. He had smooth, tanned skin. Defined cheekbones. Pale blue eyes.

Jack had short dark hair, sticky out ears and boring brown eyes. He was plain. Average. Run-of-the-mill. What he'd give to have defined cheekbones! As well as not being particularly good looking, Jack wasn't particularly athletic either. Not compared to some of the kids at school. Shakeil Baig, one of the kids in

Jack's year was a couple of feet taller and a several feet wider. He was twelve years old, the same age as Jack, but he had a body like one of the models from a bodybuilding magazine. Cora reckoned he'd been genetically engineered or something.

Jack wasn't brainy either. OK, he wasn't dumb, but he was way off the top of the class. Max Grey. Now he was top of the class. He knew the answer to everything. Apparently he already had a place lined up at Oxford. Or Cambridge. Jack wasn't sure what the difference was.

Jack thought about some of the other boys at school. Lucas Chambers was rich. He always had the latest trainers. Jack only got new trainers on special occasions like Christmas or his birthday. Tyson Schofield could play the guitar. Jack could just about play the triangle. Ben Crowe could emcee and made music videos, which he put on his own YouTube channel. Jack's lyrical abilities probably went as far as being able to rhyme 'cat' and 'mat'. Leon Walters was signed to Wolfchester Town's football academy. Jack could just about kick a ball.

What did Jack really have to offer? OK, he *did* have a good imagination and wrote loads of horror stories. He also had a pretty impressive collection of horror movie memorabilia, and he had completed *Demon Warriors* on insane difficulty setting, but who was going to be impressed with that, other than Cora?

'So you gonna do it then?' asked Cora.

'Nope,' said Jack.

'Not ever?'

'Why do you even care?'

'Because you're my bestie,' said Cora. 'I just want my bestie to be happy.'

'Really?'

'Yeah, really,' said Cora. 'Stop being so weird and just go and ask her!'

Maybe Cora was right. Chloe might like Jack back. It was possible, wasn't it? Strange things did happen sometimes. Plus, there was someone for everyone. That's what his mum said, when Jack questioned why she put up with his dad's ridiculous collection of old video games. Maybe Chloe could be for Jack? Maybe, today was his day?

'OK,' said Jack. 'I'll do it. If it'll shut you up.'

'You'll ask her out?'

Jack took in a deep breath. He nodded.

A huge grin came over Cora's face. She slapped Jack on the back. 'Go on, my son! Get yourself over there!'

# A BOLD MOVE

'Not now,' said Jack. 'I didn't mean now.'

'Why not? She's just over there.'

'But… she's with *him*.'

'Mate, she's *always* with him.'

'I know… but…'

'Just ignore him.'

Cora was right, wasn't she? Jack couldn't let Isaac stand in the way of his happiness forever, could he? Jack clenched his teeth. Then he puffed out some air. 'What will I say?' asked Jack.

'Just keep it simple. Say, "Hi Chloe. I was wondering whether you'd like to go out some time? We could go ice skating or something."'

'I hate ice skating,' said Jack. 'I'm proper rubbish at it.'

'OK, bowling.'

'Bowling's even worse. It makes your arm dead achey.'

'Well just ask her to the cinema or something then.'

'Yeah, OK, the cinema's not too bad. We could get some pick 'n' mix.'

'Yeah, pick 'n' mix.'

'Popcorn too.'

'Popcorn. Yep.'

'Maybe even…'

Cora shoved Jack in the arm. 'Just go, man!'

Jack nodded. He took another big breath. 'Right. I'm gonna do it. This is it. Right now. I'm gonna do it.' Jack looked over at Chloe, as she sat at the back of the field with that streak of lovely bright blue in her hair. 'Like bubblegum ice cream,' said Jack.

'You what?' asked Cora.

'Nothing,' mumbled Jack, embarrassed.

*You can do this*, said a positive, confident voice in his head. Then another voice appeared. It sounded like him too, but it wasn't as positive and definitely not as confident. *Can you? Can you really?*

*Yes. Yes you can.*

*If you're sure.*

'Good luck,' said Cora.

'Thanks,' said Jack. Then he took a step forwards. A step towards Chloe. A step towards his destiny. A step on his shoelace. He nearly tripped over.

Cora grabbed Jack's arm, keeping him on his feet. 'Tell Jen I saved your life.' Jen was Jack's mum. Jack hated it when Cora called his parents by their first names like they were best mates.

'And be cool,' said Cora. 'You know. Cool?'

Jack didn't really know. But he nodded anyway. He bent down and tucked his laces inside his trainers. Then he set off again. This time, he didn't trip. This time his legs and feet worked. He was walking. His thighs were trembling and knees were almost knocking, but he was walking.

Jack staggered wide of the Year Tens and their wrestling. He wondered whether it was the sun that had sent the Year Tens mad. He'd heard stories of how the sun sent dogs crazy sometimes. Maybe there was something similar going on at his school?

He ploughed on, past the brawl. Fixed his eyes on Chloe. He took a long deep breath in through his nose. He juddered a bit as the air went into his lungs. This was it. He just hoped his legs would hold out.

He watched Chloe and Isaac as they giggled to one another. Even in this weather, Isaac was still wearing his long black coat. They were staring at some thick dusty-looking book together. As he got closer, Jack's heart pumped faster. He wondered whether he might have a heart attack. Or a panic attack. Or some sort of attack. All the moisture had been sucked from his mouth and pumped into his armpits. What was he doing?

Then he was there. Standing in front of Chloe

and Isaac.

Isaac nudged Chloe as he slid the weird book into his bag.

The pair of them covered their eyes from the sun and stared up at Jack. They both had puzzled looks on their faces.

'Do you want something?' asked Isaac. His tone was off. He wasn't being friendly. Then again, Jack had never known Isaac Strong to be friendly to anyone other than Chloe.

'I was… erm… I was wondering… if… whether you'd like to…'

Isaac's face broke into a kind of suspicious sneer. He scowled at Jack and shook his head. 'If you've come here to have a go, just jog on, you jerk.'

'No… I wasn't… nothing like that.'

Chloe frowned. 'Well, what do you want?' she asked.

Jack took a breath. 'Erm… I…' Jack couldn't get his words out. It was horrible. He hadn't realised how difficult it was to talk when you had no spit in your mouth. If only he could talk through his armpits, he'd be fine!

Isaac's expression had changed. He wasn't scowling now. He was smiling slyly. 'I know what he wants. He fancies you, Chloe. That's why he's here. That's right, isn't it, Jack? Isn't it? How sad and pathetic,' mocked

Isaac. 'He's like a lost little puppy.'

'You don't, do you, Jack?' asked Chloe.

'Bless him,' said Isaac. 'Bless his little heart.' Then he laughed. It was a mean, spiteful laugh.

Jack could feel anger rising up in him now as well as embarrassment. His hands curled into fists. He was about to say something back to Isaac. Something witty, about his hair or his make-up or keeping Polos in his earlobes.

But before he could get his comeback out, he felt an arm wrap around his midriff. Then he was off. A Year Ten had him. Anthony Mason. Big, sweaty Anthony Mason. He hoisted Jack over his shoulder and bundled him over to the other Year Tens. Then he threw Jack down onto the grass. Jack winced as he hit the turf.

'Pile on!' shouted Anthony.

And that's what the idiots did. Every one of them threw themselves on top of Jack. It was horrible. Awful. He was being crushed by the sweaty idiots. What was worse though was he could hear Isaac laughing.

Fortunately for Jack, the bell rang. One by one, the Year Tens dragged themselves off him. One of them, helped Jack to his feet. 'Sorry about that,' he said. 'Just a bit of fun.'

'Yeah, great fun,' said Jack. He brushed grass

cuttings off himself and trudged away.

Cora was waiting for him at the edge of the field, a nervous grin on her face. 'So... did you ask her?'

'I don't know if you saw or not, but I didn't really get the chance,' said Jack.

'Yeah. I saw. But you went over. It's a start.'

'Brilliant,' said Jack. 'What a great start.'

# DEAR CHLOE

That evening, Jack and Cora were sat up in Jack's bedroom. Jack's bedroom was probably his most favourite place in the world. It was where Jack kept his horror collection. From a young age, Jack had been fascinated with horror. Books, movies, video games – he loved it all, as long as it was scary. He had posters and figurines, and best of all, he had a shelf up on his wall, stuffed with horror masks, each stuck on the head of a mannequin. He had a devil, a skull, a zombie, a troll, and a werewolf. Some people might have found Jack's room a bit weird with all the creepy toys and masks, but Jack thought it was awesome.

Cora sat on Jack's bed with an Xbox controller in her hands, playing *Kings of Dread*.

Jack was at his desk, with his tabby cat, Lloyd, on his lap. He stroked Lloyd as he watched Cora charge about a dilapidated mansion, swinging a chainsaw around.

'This game's awesome,' grinned Cora.

'If you had to fight demons in real life,' said Jack. 'What would you use as a weapon?'

'This chainsaw's pretty good,' said Cora.

'In real life though? It's a bit heavy, don't you think? Dangerous too. Did you ever hear that story about that guy who was cutting down a tree or something, and ended up sawing off his own head?'

Cora paused the game. She stared at Jack. 'No way.'

'Serious,' said Jack. 'I read it online.'

Cora blinked. 'Maybe I'd choose a gun then. A big one though.'

'Yeah, obviously. It would have to be big.'

'Obviously.' Cora smirked. 'I was thinking…'

'Uh-oh.'

'What you saying "uh-oh" for?'

'I never like it when you're thinking!'

'What, I'm a good thinker. You should write Chloe a letter.'

Jack's face twisted up like he was sucking on something sour. 'What like a love letter?'

'Well, not necessarily a love letter. Just a letter. You could say you think she's really nice or whatever, and you'd like to take her to the prom. At least that way Isaac wouldn't be in your face and she could just read it. Plus, you're good at writing. You could make it really cool and that.'

Jack thought about his friend's suggestion. It wasn't

a bad idea. 'I could email her.'

'Yeah,' said Cora. 'Or send her a letter.'

'Who writes letters though?' asked Jack. 'Old people. And people in prison.'

'Bet you Chloe would like a letter.'

'You reckon?'

'She's got one of those faces.'

Jack wasn't exactly sure what Cora was on about, but he had heard his dad talking about letters being a dying art form. Maybe a letter could be a thing? Chloe definitely wasn't a fan of the norm.

Jack pulled open a drawer and took out a pad of lined A4 paper. He gently picked Lloyd up from his lap and put the cat down on the floor. 'Gotta do some work, Lloydy,' he said. 'Hope you understand.'

'You doing it then?' asked Cora.

'Couldn't hurt to at least write something,' said Jack. 'Not like I have to send it, is it?'

Lloyd meowed and leapt up onto the bed. He curled himself into a ball and closed his eyes.

'So what should I start it with?' asked Jack.

'Dear Chloe…' said Cora.

'You reckon?'

'That's how you start letters isn't it? Or maybe you should write your address and that in the corner. And the date. That's what you do isn't it?'

Jack rubbed his head. The only letter he could ever

remember writing was when he was little, offering Father Christmas somewhere to live because he was worried about the North Pole melting.

Jack plucked a pen out of his pen pot and wrote his address in the top right corner. Then he wrote, 'Dear Chloe'.

'So what else do I put?' asked Jack.

'Just say what you want to say. You're the writer. Write!'

So that's what Jack did. He was honest and wrote what he felt. It took him about ten minutes to write the letter. When he was done, he read it back to Cora. It went like this:

Dear Chloe,

I hope you don't mind me writing you a letter. I know you might think it's lame or something, but it's a dying art form and I know you like art. Anyway, it's hard to talk sometimes when there's no spit in your mouth, so I thought writing my thoughts down would be better. Here goes.

I really like you. I liked you from the first day I saw you at school. I think your hair is awesome. I think your nose stud is really cool. And I think your boots make you look like you could kick my butt! I think you're the coolest girl in school and

# DON'T FEED THE TROLL!

I'd really like to hang out with you some time. We could go ice-skating if you want, even though I'm rubbish at it. Or we could go bowling, even though it makes my arm all achey. Or we could go to the cinema. I like horror films best. I have an amazing collection of horror figures and masks. You might think they're cool. I like writing horror stories too. You could read one if you like. I've also completed Demon Warriors on INSANE. It took me ages and was really hard.

Anyway, if you'd like to go to the prom with me, please let me know. You can circle one of the options below and return this letter to me.

Yes I'd love to go to the prom with you!

I'll think about it and get back to you.

No, I wouldn't like to go to the prom with you, but I'll keep your letter to myself and never ever tell anyone about it.

Yours hopefully,
Jack Gosling

Jack was pretty pleased with it. He hoped Cora would think it was good too. 'What do you think?'

'Hmmm. Well it's honest, I guess,' said Cora. 'But do you have to talk about the masks and *Demon Warriors*?'

'But she likes horror stuff too, doesn't she?' asked Jack.

'I don't know what she likes,' said Cora.

Jack didn't really know either. He just assumed she did, as she always wore black like a Goth. Goths liked horror stuff. Jack was pretty certain about that. He was probably a Goth underneath his normal clothes and boring face. 'Do you think I should take that out?' asked Jack.

Cora nodded. 'It makes you sound a bit weird.'

'But I am a bit weird,' said Jack.

'Let her find that out for herself,' grinned Cora.

Jack took another piece of paper from the pad and started writing again. This time he left out the bits about his horror figures and masks and *Demon Warriors*.

'Right,' said Cora. 'Let's go post it!'

# A LOVE LETTER

The pair of them raced down the stairs.

'I'm just popping out,' shouted Jack. 'I'll be five minutes.'

'Tea'll be ready in half an hour,' shouted Jack's mum. 'Don't be late!'

'I won't!' Jack shouted back. Then he opened the door and hurried outside. Cora followed him.

Outside it was still warm. The smell of a neighbour's barbecue filled Jack's nose and made his belly rumble. It didn't feel right delivering a letter like this in broad daylight. It felt like it should have been a sneaky mission. Jack wondered whether he should wait until after dark to do it, but he knew if he did, he might not do it at all. And as scared as he was of Chloe telling him where to stick his letter, he *did* want to hang out with her. As his dad always said, 'If you don't buy a ticket, you won't win the raffle.' This letter was Jack's ticket. Chloe was the star prize at the raffle. Much better than any radio alarm clock or bottle of bubble bath.

Jack and Cora turned left onto March Road, then left again onto Westchester Avenue. Jack knew where Chloe lived because he'd seen her walk home after school. He always made sure to hang back so that it didn't seem like he was following her. It wasn't like he was actually following her anyway. He had to go the same way. But he sort of *was* following her. In a way. Because he liked looking at her. He was glad he'd taken the horror stuff out of his letter now. If she'd read that, then seen him following her home after school, who knows what she'd have thought?

And then they were outside Chloe's house – number sixty-three. It was a normal looking house, just like all the other houses on the street. When Jack had first seen where Chloe lived, he was a little surprised. He thought that a girl as unique as Chloe should probably live somewhere really cool like a fun fair or a lighthouse. But she didn't. She lived in a semi-detached house with double-glazing and a silver car parked on the drive.

'You OK?' asked Cora.

'I'm OK,' said Jack.

Cora smiled. 'Go on then.'

Jack nodded. He walked up Chloe's driveway, past the silver car. He stopped at the front door and looked at the envelope. It was plain white. He'd got it from his dad's study. He'd written 'Chloe' on the front. Or the back. He was never sure which way round was which with envelopes.

He heard Chloe shouting from inside the house. Then a boy shouted something back. It sounded like they were arguing. It was probably Chloe's younger brother, Mark. He was in the year below Jack at school.

Jack wondered whether posting a letter was such a good idea after all. If everyone at school found out, it could be the end of him. He'd be known as 'Love Letter Boy' for the rest of his life. Something like that – you might never get over it.

But if he didn't post it, he'd never win the raffle. He'd never get to hang out with Chloe. And how cool would that be?

He stared at the letter some more. He didn't want to let go of it. He was too scared. Who knew what might happen once it was sent?

*Just do it*, said the confident voice in his head.

*Wait*, said the scared voice.

*Do it*, said the confident voice. *DO IT DO IT DO IT…*

Jack shoved the letter through the letterbox. And as soon as it left his fingers, he knew.

He'd just made the biggest mistake of his life.

# A MASSIVE MISTAKE

The letterbox banged.

Jack's eyes sprang open. He looked up at the clock. It was just after seven in the morning.

Jack threw off his duvet and jumped out of bed. He slipped his feet into his Bigfoot slippers and raced onto the landing. He paused at the top of the stairs. There was something on the mat in the hallway.

A white envelope.

This was it.

Chloe had read his letter and replied. OK, she was an early bird, which was surprising, but maybe she couldn't wait to tell him she wanted to hang out!

Then again, maybe she couldn't wait to tell him to get lost.

Not as awesome. Pretty rubbish, actually.

Jack charged down the stairs. At least he would know. One way or the other, he would know if there was any chance of Chloe and him happening. He bent over, scooped the letter up. Then he sniffed it. He thought Chloe might have sprayed it with perfume or something. He'd seen a girl do it in some film. It didn't smell of perfume though. It smelt of paper. And when he really thought about it, he didn't imagine Chloe was the sort of girl who'd spray anything with perfume. Except maybe the eyes of burglars, if they had the nerve to break into her house.

He turned the letter over expecting to see the word 'Jack'. There was no Jack. There was just some printed label addressed to Jack's dad.

All of the everything Jack had built up inside him – the excitement, the nerves – it all disappeared with a big sigh. All he felt now was disappointment.

Jack's dad appeared in the living room doorway. He was wearing a Homer Simpson T-shirt and his Wolfchester Town shorts. He had Bigfoot slippers on too. His brown hair was all over the place and he was all stubbly. He was holding two mugs. One that said 'Pat', which was his. The other said 'Jen', which was Jack's mum's. Jack had one as well.

Jack's dad saw the letter in Jack's hand and frowned. 'You expecting something?' asked Jack's dad.

'Not really,' said Jack.

'I don't like the sound of "not really".'

'OK then. No. I'm not expecting anything.'

'I hope you haven't ordered anything. You remember what happened the last time?'

# A MASSIVE MISTAKE

Jack thought about the 'last time' his dad was referring too. Jack had found the most awesome *Kings of Dread* figure. He bid on it using his dad's account. Way more than he should've. Ended up paying three times what it was worth. He'd only just finished paying it back out of his pocket money.

'It's OK, Dad,' said Jack. 'I haven't ordered anything.'

'Good. And you better not.'

Jack groaned.

'Everything all right, son?'

'Yep,' lied Jack. He trudged back upstairs.

Jack and Cora took their seats at the back of their form room. They were usually the first to get into class, other than David Meredith and a couple of others, who sat up at the front.

'So, did you hear anything back?' asked Cora.

Jack shook his head.

'Don't worry,' said Cora. 'Early days.'

Other kids started coming into class.

'What happened to you yesterday?' Tyson Schofield asked Jack. 'Heard you got smacked down by Anthony Mason.'

'Just a bit of fun,' said Jack.

Tyson laughed. 'Yeah, man. I bet it was. Gettin' all hot and sweaty with Masher Mason!'

Jack didn't bother saying anything back. He just pretended to laugh along.

Cora nudged Jack.

Chloe appeared in the classroom, followed as ever, by Isaac.

Jack swallowed. He looked away. 'Is she looking over?' he whispered to Cora.

'I don't think so,' said Cora.

'You don't think so?'

'OK. No.'

Jack glanced over at Chloe and Isaac. He studied Chloe for any sign that she'd read his letter. Chloe didn't look at Jack. Instead, she whispered and laughed with Isaac. Just like always. Jack sometimes wondered what Chloe would be like if she didn't hang around with Isaac. He thought she might actually get along with everyone. It was Isaac. He was the problem.

Then Isaac looked over at Jack and gave Jack a seriously odd smile. He'd seen the letter. There was no doubting it. Chloe had read the letter, shown it to Isaac and Jack was now the butt of their jokes.

Jack was mortified. His heart beat fast. They could've done anything with it. They could've photocopied it and put it up all around school. They could've posted it online. Isaac was some kind of computer whiz and he was evil enough to devote an entire website to such a thing.

# A MASSIVE MISTAKE

Jack suddenly wished he could undo what he'd done. He wished he could suck it all back up inside him and just keep it there. He wished he could sell his raffle ticket. He didn't want even want to be entered. He'd definitely made a mistake – a massive Anthony Mason-sized mistake.

# TROLL BOY

The next week was horrible. Every time Jack heard a letter drop on the mat, he'd spring into life, hoping Chloe had finally responded. Each day at school, he'd be watching the pair, looking for a hint of what they were planning, and each day nothing became any clearer. He'd check the noticeboards as he passed them in the school corridor. He scoured Chloe and Isaac's social media, looking for any mention of him or his letter. And with every day that passed, Jack's disappointment grew, and began to fester into something he didn't quite recognise. He started to feel resentful and angry. OK, being ridiculed for his letter would've been horrible. But at least it would've been acknowledgement. He felt so unimportant. So irrelevant. Like he wasn't even worth bothering with. It was like he was no one.

A few weeks after Jack had posted the letter, Jack and Cora were in Jack's bedroom. Cora was playing *Kings of Dread* while Jack was online.

'Still haven't found anything,' said Jack. 'I don't get why they're leaving it so long.'

'Maybe they're not planning anything,' said Cora.

'What do you mean?'

'Just that maybe they're not planning anything. Maybe she never read the letter.'

'How could she not have?' asked Jack. ''Course she did.'

'I dunno. Anyway, you tried didn't you? That's more than some people would've done. You should be pleased with yourself.'

'Yeah right.' Jack sighed. 'They're planning something, I know it.'

'Just forget about it,' said Cora. 'Let it go.'

That was the thing. Jack couldn't forget about it. He couldn't let it go. He wished he could. But he just couldn't. He thought about it loads. He thought about how he'd put his feelings into that letter and now he felt vulnerable and paranoid and stupid and angry at himself. His head was so full of Chloe and Isaac and anger and embarrassment, he couldn't concentrate on anything else. He had to *do* something.

'I'm going to get them,' said Jack.

'What you on about?' Cora's tongue hung from her mouth as she sliced through a demon with a chainsaw.

'Chloe and Isaac think they're all that, don't they,' said Jack.

'Guess.'

'You know, they're always whispering and laughing at people behind their backs like they're so amazing.'

'Isaac does.'

'But Chloe goes along with it. That makes her just as bad. If it was a crime, she'd be charged too. She'd be an accessory.'

'What, like a hat?'

'Not a fashion accessory. An accessory to a crime.'

'Ring the police then,' said Cora.

'I'm gonna do better than that,' said Jack.

Jack loaded up his social media page and created a new account, calling himself 'Troll Boy'. He then typed 'troll' into Google. One of the images that came up caught his eye. It was a black and white picture of a wide face with a big mischievous grin. Its eyes were small and squinting and it had worry lines and big teeth. Perfect. He copied it and uploaded it as his profile picture.

'Troll Boy,' said Jack.

Cora paused the game and rolled over the bed. She stared at the monitor and shrugged. 'What you on about – Troll Boy?'

'I'm gonna give them a taste of their own medicine. See how they like it.'

'Who?'

'Chloe and Isaac.'

'You still on about that?'

Jack just glared at her.

'What you gonna do?' asked Cora.

'Just watch!'

In a flash, Jack had found Isaac and Chloe's accounts.

'Look at some of the rubbish they write,' said Jack. ' "Today I saw a dead bird. It was beautiful." '

'Who's put that?' asked Cora.

'Isaac. Who d'you think?'

Jack typed a comment of his own:

NO ONE CARES, YOU FREAK

His finger hovered over the reply button.

'Shall I?' he asked Cora.

'You can't.'

'Can't I?' A mischievous smile appeared on Jack's face. He pressed the button. The pair watched as Jack's comment appeared under Isaac's 'dead bird' post.

'No way,' said Cora. 'Can't believe you just did that!'

'This is just the start!' said Jack.

For the next ten minutes, Jack fired comment after comment at Isaac and Chloe. He mocked their dumb posts. He mocked their spelling mistakes. He mocked their eyeliner and hair and clothes and earlobes. He mocked and mocked and mocked and the more he mocked, the more his anger and disappointment seemed to seep away from him.

There was a knock at the door. Jack's dad stuck his head in. 'What are you pair up to?' he asked.

Jack switched internet pages quickly to a horror magazine homepage. 'Just looking at some funny stuff,' said Jack.

'Better not be rude,' said Jack's dad.

'As if!' said Jack.

'All right then. Do you want anything?'

'I'm good,' Jack replied.

'I'll have a cuppa, Pat, if that's OK?' asked Cora.

Jack's dad smiled. 'That's fine, Cora. Two sugars?'

'Yes please, Pat.'

'And you, Jack? Fancy a cuppa?' asked Jack's dad.

'Go on then,' said Jack.

'Right you are. Give me five minutes.' Jack's dad disappeared, closing the door behind him.

'Do you have to call my dad 'Pat'?' asked Jack.

'What? That's his name,' said Cora.

'I know. It's just weird,' said Jack.

'You're weird,' said Cora. 'Now have a look. See if they've said anything back.'

The pair of them grinned at one another.

# TROLL BOY

Jack clicked onto his social media page.

There it was. A reply from Isaac:

I DONT KNO WHO THIS IS, BUT I'LL FIND U &
I'LL GET U!

'Do you think he'll actually do something?' asked
Cora.

'As if,' said Jack.

'But everyone calls them witches,' said Cora. 'What
if they put a spell on us? Something bad?'

Jack stared at Cora. 'You being serious?'

Cora stared back. Then burst out laughing. 'As if!'

Jack laughed too, but less loud than his friend.
Because Cora had planted the idea in Jack's head.

What if Isaac and Chloe *did* do something bad?

# FOLLOWERS

When Jack and Cora got into their classroom the next day, a few kids were huddled around David Meredith's mobile phone, whispering to one another. They seemed excited. There was a bit of a buzz.

Jack and Cora took their seat at the back of the class. Jack let his bag slide off his shoulder and onto the floor.

David Meredith and his mates laughed.

Jack nudged Cora. 'What's up with that lot?' she asked.

Cora shrugged.

'Oi,' said Jack. 'What're you lot doing?'

'Someone called Troll Boy,' said David Meredith. He was a skinny kid with dark, curly hair and round glasses. He scratched the back of his hand. He had pretty bad eczema. 'He's been winding Isaac and Chloe up. It's pretty funny!'

'Don't you reckon that's a bit mean?' asked Jack.

'No way,' said David Meredith. 'They're horrible

to everyone. They deserve it.'

Jack smiled. David Meredith was right. Isaac and Chloe *did* deserve it. Not only was he making himself feel better, but he was doing everyone else a service. Troll Boy was one of the good guys.

'I reckon it's Tyson,' said David Meredith.

'Tyson?' asked Cora. 'Why?'

'I just do,' said David Meredith. 'Only someone like him would have the guts to do it.'

'As if!' said Jack.

'Well who do you think it is?' asked David Meredith.

'Could be anyone,' said Jack. 'Could be someone in this room.'

David Meredith raised his bushy eyebrows. He looked at his mates, then at Jack and Cora. He scratched the back of his hand again. 'Don't think so.'

'You never know though, do you?' asked Jack.

Cora poked Jack in the knee under the table. 'It's probably someone else though isn't it,' said Cora. 'Probably someone in Year Ten or something. That lot are always doing stupid stuff like that.'

Chloe and Isaac entered the classroom.

Everyone went quiet. David Meredith slipped his phone into his pocket.

There was a scowl on Isaac's face. He didn't look happy at all.

Jack knew he was the one who'd put the scowl on Isaac's face. He felt like he'd won for once. But it was a bit scary. Jack hadn't ever stuck his neck out like this. OK, he couldn't stand Isaac. Not only was Isaac always with Chloe, which was annoying, Isaac was mean to everyone. But then if Jack was doing the same thing to Isaac as he did to everyone else, did that make him just as bad?

A sickly feeling settled in Jack's belly.

'What are you staring at, you freak?' Isaac asked Jack.

Jack hadn't even realised he *was* staring.

'Do you want a picture or something?'

Jack snarled at Isaac, but didn't say anything. The sick feeling in his belly went away. Instead, his stomach acids started bubbling. He was glad he'd done what he'd done. Isaac really was horrible. He deserved everything he got and then some.

At break, Jack and Cora went up to the computer lab. Miss George, the computing teacher, let the kids she liked use the PCs as long as they were well behaved. Jack could be cheeky sometimes, but most of the teachers seemed to like him.

Jack sat at a PC and logged on.

Cora sat at the PC next to him. She didn't log on.

Jack took a look around the classroom to see if

anyone was watching. Miss George was talking to David Meredith about some science documentary, but no one was paying any attention to Jack. He logged into his Troll Boy account.

He had over a hundred followers already. He blinked. Then he nudged Cora. 'Check this out. A hundred followers.'

'A hundred?' asked Cora. 'That's loads.'

'I should post something,' said Jack. 'For my fans.'

'Go on then,' said Cora.

Jack typed another message for Isaac.

HOPE UR MASCARA DIDN'T RUN FROM ALL THE CRYING U MUST'VE DONE LAST NITE!

Cora laughed. 'You gonna send it?'

'Of course.'

Jack pressed 'send'. 'I was thinking,' he said. 'We should take it to the next level.'

Cora frowned. 'What next level?'

'We should make a video.'

'About what?'

'I could dress up as Troll Boy,' said Jack. 'I could *tell* Isaac and Chloe what I really think.'

'Why would you do that?'

'Why wouldn't I?'

'Well they might recognise you – or your voice or

something?'

'They wouldn't.'

'They might,' said Cora.

'I've got this editing software. I'd change my voice and that. Can you imagine how cool it'd be? I'd be like a hero or something!'

Cora shook her head. 'How would you?'

'I'd be Troll Boy, telling people like it is. Everyone would love me.'

'I think you should stick with your messages,' said Cora.

'Don't be such a little chicken,' said Jack.

'I'm not a little chicken.'

'You are. A little baby chicken. Chick chick chick chick chickarrrrn…'

Cora scowled at Jack. 'Just shut up.'

'Whatever,' said Jack and he refreshed his page. He had two more followers. 'I'm gonna make a video,' he said. 'Whether you help me or not.'

# ACTION!

All day long, Jack was checking his phone for new followers. When he got home from school that afternoon, he was straight into his bedroom, setting the place up ready for his video. He didn't need any flash equipment to record himself – he had his phone. It wasn't amazing quality or anything, but it was good enough for Jack.

There was a knock at the front door.

'I'll get it!' shouted Jack, as he raced downstairs. The thought of Chloe delivering her reply darted through Jack's mind, but he realised that was silly. That was all done with. There'd never be any reply. It was time to forget about all that and move on. Jack had a new project: Project Troll Boy.

He turned the catch and opened the door.

Cora was there. 'You ready to do this video?' she asked.

'Shhhh,' said Jack. 'Not so loud.'

Cora mouthed the word 'sorry'.

The pair of them scurried up the stairs and into Jack's bedroom. Jack closed the door behind them.

'I was thinking I should sit in my chair,' said Jack. 'You can film me from my bed?' He handed her his phone.

'Cool. So I'm like the director?' asked Cora.

Jack frowned and shrugged.

'Go on,' said Cora. 'Let me be the director. I've always wanted to be a director.'

'Since when?' asked Jack.

Cora shook her head. 'I dunno. Since… now!'

'Do you even know what a director does?' asked Jack.

Cora shook her head again.

'All right, whatever,' said Jack. 'Just film when I tell you to.'

Jack hurried over to his shelf filled with masks and pulled the troll mask off its mannequin head. It was dark green with big sticky-out ears. There were two holes for eyes and a tuft of hair on top. Two tusk-like teeth stuck up from its jaw and over its top lip, either side of its thick nose. It was a hideous-looking thing. One of Jack's favourites. He pulled it over his head.

'How do I look?' asked Jack.

'Very pretty,' said Cora.

Jack snickered and sat in his chair.

# ACTION!

'D'you even know what you're gonna say?' asked Cora.

'Got an idea,' said Jack. 'But I'll just make it up as I go along. If it's rubbish, we can do it again. Start recording.'

'I think I'm the one who has to decide when I start recording,' said Cora. 'I am the director after all.'

'Just start,' said Jack.

'OK,' said Cora. 'ACTION!'

Jack shook his head. 'What you saying that for?'

'It's what directors say, isn't it?'

Jack shook his head all over again.

'*ACTION* then!'

'Chill out,' said Jack. He took a breath. 'Hello everyone,' he said in this weird trolly voice. 'I'm Troll Boy and I'm here to tell it like it is…'

'Erm… Jack…' said Cora.

'What?'

'Don't think it's recording,' said Cora. 'How d'you use this thing?'

'You're useless.' Jack stomped over to Cora and grabbed the his phone from her. 'Here, see this button?' He pointed to a large red button on the camera app.

'Uh-huh,' said Cora.

'Press that,' said Jack.

'Press that,' repeated Cora. 'Got it.'

'Seriously, Cor.' Jack shook his head as he went back over to his seat.

'Right,' said Cora. 'You good?'

'Let's do this!' said Jack.

Cora pressed the red button hard, making extra sure it was on. 'Right, looks good. ACTION!'

'Hello everyone,' said Jack in his trolly voice. 'I'm Troll Boy and I'm here to tell it like it is.'

'This is good,' said Cora.

'Shhh!'

'Sorry.'

'First off,' said Jack. 'I'd like to say a special hello to Isaac Strong and Chloe Jones. Two of my favourite people. So, Isaac, you're going to get me, you say. Well, you're going to have to find me first. I could be anywhere. I could be outside your house. I mean, not now, obviously. I'm in the troll cave right now. But later, when I'm done here, I could creep into your house and get *you*. Just think, next time you're putting on your make-up, I might be watching you. Trolls can do that sort of thing, you know. They can creep around and that.'

'Can they?' asked Cora.

'Shhh!'

'Oh yeah, sorry,' whispered Cora.

'So remember, Isaac,' said Jack. 'It might be *you* who gets got first! Troll you later!' Jack gave it a few seconds before he said 'CUT!' Then he pulled the troll mask off. His face was hot and sweaty. He rubbed his hair. 'Pass me my phone, Cor,' he said.

Cora handed Jack his phone.

Jack opened the video file to check it was there. It was. He pressed play. It looked and sounded pretty decent.

'You *sure* this is a good idea?' asked Cora.

'Yeah,' said Jack. 'It's a great idea.'

Cora screwed her face up.

'Why are you screwing your face up?' asked Jack. 'You're not going all baby chick chick again are you?'

'What if they find out it's you?' asked Cora. 'They might call the police or something?'

'What would the police do? It's not against the law to wear a troll mask is it?'

'But saying mean things about people might be,' said Cora. 'Isn't that like slander or something?'

'It's fine. Trust me. People are going to love this!'

Cora smiled, unsure.

Jack could see from her face that Cora didn't seem like she trusted Jack at all with this.

# MUM AND DAD

Jack edited the footage, removing Cora's interruptions as well as adding in some sound effects and a few pictures of Isaac and Chloe he found online. He distorted his voice too, making it deep and slow, so no one would ever guess it was him who was talking. He even put in a title card. TROLL BOY – EPISODE 1. Cora was a little disappointed she didn't get any credit for her directorial début, but it was either that or tell the whole world who was responsible for Troll Boy. Once Jack was happy with his creation, he uploaded it.

'Are you *totally* sure this is a good idea?' asked Cora.

'How many times? Yes!'

'But once something's online, you don't know who'll get their hands on it, do you?'

'So?' Jack shrugged, as he posted lots of links to the video, paying special attention to make sure Isaac and Chloe got wind of it.

'Maybe you should just go and talk to her,' said

Cora. 'Ask her why she didn't reply to your letter, instead of… all this.'

'Talk to her?' asked Jack in disbelief. 'Are you mad?'

'What's mad about that? Seems like the most sensible thing to do to me.'

'What do you know about anything?' snapped Jack.

Cora didn't say anything back. But not long after, she went home. Jack was sorry for being mean, but he didn't apologise. Cora was putting doubts in his mind and Jack had enough of those as it was. He needed someone to back him, fill him with confidence, tell him he was doing the right thing. Because he was doing the right thing: wiping the smug smiles from Isaac and Chloe's faces. That was the right thing.

Wasn't it?

Jack turned off his laptop and trudged downstairs.

His mum was on the sofa in the living room. Her hair was tied back and she was wearing a hoodie that said Wolfchester University on it. She was typing up notes on her laptop, a pile of textbooks beside her. Jack's mum was a social worker. She worked with kids in care. She seemed to like her job, even if she did whine about the paperwork and stress most of the time.

'Hi, Jack,' she said. 'Has Cora gone?'

'Yeah, just now,' said Jack, trying not to think

about Cora and her niggling doubts.

Jack sat next to his mum and watched as she typed away. 'Busy day?' he asked.

'Is there any other kind? Your dad's down in the basement,' said Jack's mum. 'He's testing out some stuff.'

'You mean playing rubbish old games!' said Jack.

Jack's mum smiled. 'Yeah, he's playing rubbish old games.'

'Don't you ever get annoyed with him?' asked Jack.

'Always.'

Jack smiled. 'So why do you put up with it?'

'That's what you do when you love someone,' she said.

'Is it?'

'I think so.'

'How did you know you loved Dad?' asked Jack. 'At first, I mean? You know… when you first realised?'

'Good question.' She stopped typing. 'I guess I didn't realise it for a while. Then one day, he went away on holiday with his friends. And I didn't want him to go. And the whole time he was away, I felt sick.'

'Really?'

'Weird, isn't it?'

'A bit.'

'When he came back, I stopped feeling sick,' she

said. 'And he's never been away from me since.'

Jack doubted Chloe would feel sick if he left. She hadn't even bothered to reply to his letter. Her feelings were pretty clear.

'Anyway,' said his mum. 'Why are you asking? You're not one for lovely-dovey nonsense.'

'I was just interested,' said Jack.

'You're like your dad. Not a romantic bone in your bodies, the pair of you.'

Jack frowned. 'I might be romantic.'

'Really?'

'I dunno.' Jack thought about the letter he'd written for Chloe. That was pretty romantic, wasn't it? But then look how that had turned out. Maybe that was why his dad wasn't romantic. Maybe he'd tried to be at some point and he'd just been ignored or had it thrown back in his face.

'Jack,' said his mum. 'Is there a girl on the scene?'

'No,' said Jack. 'What scene?'

'The love scene – it's what people say.'

'There's no girl.'

'Or a boy. That's fine too.'

'There's no one!'

Jack's mum smiled and nudged him with her leg. 'I know you, Jack. You don't ask questions like this without something going on. Well, if there is a girl… or a boy… they'd be very lucky to have you in their lives.'

'Yeah, right,' said Jack.

'Hey, lovely lad, come here.'

Jack's mum always called him things like 'lovely lad' or 'angel' or 'baby boy'. It made Jack cringe a bit, but he sort of liked it too.

His mum put her arm around him and gave him a squeeze. 'Now, I can tell you exactly when I fell in love with you…'

'Really, mum?' groaned Jack. 'Do you have to?'

'No. But I will.' She grinned. 'The very first time I laid eyes on you. That's when I knew I loved you. You were so small. So precious.'

Jack poked his fingers into his mouth and pretended to gag.

'It's OK for you to talk about your feelings you know,' she said.

'I know,' said Jack.

'I mean it,' she went on, and she sounded like she *really* meant it.

'I know,' Jack repeated, sounding like he really knew.

'Now,' said his mum. 'Why don't you go and tell your dad I'm hungry.'

'OK, sure. Just don't tell anyone what I'm about to say,' said Jack.

His mum looked at him, frowning. 'OK?'

'Love you.'

She smiled. 'I know you do, baby boy.'

Jack smiled too. He left his mum to her notes and crept down the stairs into the basement. Or the 'Dad Cave' as his dad called it.

The Dad Cave was a pretty impressive sight, even to someone like Jack, who didn't really care much for old stuff. There were shelves everywhere and they were all packed with old action figures and toys and video games. There was a Nintendo shelf, a Sega shelf, an Atari shelf and shelves with games for video games systems Jack couldn't even pronounce. It was easy to see where Jack got his collecting streak from. His dad was the biggest collector out there – or down there – in the basement. His dad bought and sold this stuff for a living. He didn't seem to do badly out of it either, which always surprised Jack. Jack couldn't believe some of the money people paid for old junk. But as his dad always said, 'one man's trash, another man's treasure.'

His dad was sat on a sofa, playing an old video game.

'What you playing?' asked Jack.

'*Super Mario World*,' said Jack's dad. 'And I'm *testing* it. Not playing. A vital part of the job,' he said with a grin.

'Yeah, right,' said Jack. He sat next to his dad.

'Mum said she's hungry.'

'I'll be up in a minute.'

'So it works OK?' asked Jack, pointing at the TV screen.

'It does. Best to be thorough though. You can never quite tell.'

Jack smiled. 'How many times have you clocked this?'

'Twenty-three at the last count.'

'You're such a geek,' said Jack.

'Takes one to know one!'

They both laughed.

Jack watched as Super Mario jumped on the heads of cute-looking creatures. Then he mistimed a jump and fell down a gap between platforms. Jack's dad smiled at him and handed him the joy pad. 'You're up, sunshine.'

Jack took the pad from his dad and completed the level with ease.

'You've got your dad's skills all right!' smiled his dad.

'You should play some *Kings of Dread* with me.'

'Not for me, son, I'm afraid. 'I'm a simple man of simple means. Sixteen bits is about my limit.'

'But these graphics are terrible!' said Jack.

'This was state of the art, when I was your age,' said his dad.

'Yeah, maybe in 1853!'

'How old do you think I am?' asked Jack's dad.

'Sixty-something?'

Jack's dad shoved him in the arm. 'You're getting way too cheeky, kid. Actually, you always were. Remember how you used to blame all your cheek on your imaginary friend when you were little – what was he called?'

'Pongo.'

'Pongo, that's the one,' said Jack's dad. 'Pongo the penguin. Used to get you in all sorts of mischief, didn't he?'

Jack smiled. 'Yeah.'

'You've always had the most amazing imagination,' said Jack's dad.

'Pat, are you making tea or what?' shouted Jack's mum from upstairs.

'In a minute,' his dad shouted back. 'Just one more life,' he whispered. He took the pad from Jack and unpaused the game.

After tea, Jack went back to his room. He turned on his laptop and waited for it to boot up. As soon as it did, he checked his page. His Troll Boy video had over a hundred views already and loads of comments. Most of them were positive too, with people posting things like 'I love Troll Boy' and 'Troll Boy is awesomeness!' Jack couldn't believe it. It was soooooo cool! His followers had doubled too. He had over two hundred now. He tried to work out how many followers he'd get by the end of the year if they doubled every day. He stopped after a while because it started to hurt his brain. He wasn't much good at maths, to be fair.

Another thought came to him. What if his followers *did* double every day? How would he keep them all happy? It was a big responsibility. And surely, the more people that knew about him, the bigger chance there was of someone uncovering his true identity? Jack had hidden his face and disguised his voice. He'd covered his tracks pretty well as far as he was concerned. But what if he'd forgot something? What if he'd left a vital clue?

What if people found out Jack was Troll Boy?

# THE FALL OUT

For the next few nights, Jack did exactly the same thing. As soon as he got home from school, he'd open up his social media account and post loads of insulting things about Isaac and Chloe. And every day at school, Isaac's scowl grew darker. He became quieter and less annoying. Chloe was quiet too. They didn't seem to whisper and laugh at people anymore, instead everyone was whispering and laughing at them. Jack's followers grew too. OK, they didn't quite double every day, but within a few days he over three hundred followers. Jack was pretty pleased with himself.

'Got over three hundred now, Cor,' said Jack.

Cora was lying on Jack's bed, staring up at the ceiling. 'Great.'

'Don't you think that's good?' asked Jack.

'I said 'great'.'

'Yeah, but you don't sound like you mean it.'

'You're right, Jack. It's getting boring.'

'How is it?'

'It's all you ever talk about. Who cares how many followers you've got? You've taken this all way too far.'

'You're just jealous!'

'Yeah, right.'

'You are. People are interested in me.'

'They're not interested in *you* though, are they,' said Cora. 'They're interested in Troll Boy.'

'That *is* me.'

'Whatever. I think you're getting obsessed.'

'What do you know,' grumbled Jack.

'Exactly. What do I know? Dumb old Cora doesn't know anything.'

'You said it,' said Jack.

Cora rolled into a sitting position. 'I'm going.'

'Suit yourself.'

Cora left the room.

'Idiot,' whispered Jack. He refreshed his page. Another follower. Another person interested in seeing what Troll Boy did next. Cora was wrong. Jack wasn't obsessed. He just had a project, that was all. Troll Boy gave Jack something to put his energy into. It was either that or skulk about feeling sorry for himself because Chloe had knocked him back.

Jack folded his arms and sat back in his chair. Then he leaned forwards and refreshed his page again. No new followers.

# THE FALL OUT

The next morning, Jack waited for Cora until 8:40 am, but Cora didn't come. He'd figured that she wouldn't, but he thought he'd at least give her a chance. Jack hoisted his backpack over his shoulder.

His mum came out of the kitchen, eating a banana. 'Where's Cora?' she asked.

Jack shrugged. 'She must be off sick.'

'Weird,' said his mum. 'She usually lets you know, doesn't she?'

'Must've forgot,' said Jack.

'You better get off anyway, sweetheart, or you'll be late.'

Jack nodded. He kissed his mum and left.

Cora was already at their desk when Jack got into class. David Meredith and his mates were all there talking about Troll Boy's exploits from the previous night.

Jack thought about sitting at another table, but he didn't. Jack and Cora had been friends since… well… forever. He didn't really want to fall out properly with her.

'All right?' asked Jack.

'All right,' said Cora.

Jack sat down and let his bag slide to the floor. 'I waited for you this morning.'

'Did you?'

'You could've let me know you weren't coming,' said Jack.

'Sorry.'

Jack pulled a deep breath in through his nose. He could tell Cora wasn't sorry at all.

The other kids started piling into the classroom.

Isaac and Chloe entered. Chloe had dark semi-circles under her eyes. Isaac's eyes were wide.

Jack smiled at Chloe.

Chloe frowned at him. They'd never be boyfriend and girlfriend. He had to face it. He had to move on. Not just pretend he was moving on and not moving on at all. *Really* move on. She'd never love him the way his mum loved his dad. In fact, she'd hate him if she ever found out he was Troll Boy.

Isaac gave Jack a dirty look.

Jack looked away. After a few seconds, he looked back over at them. They both had their heads in their hands and seemed properly miserable. Every now and again, Isaac would have a quick look around to see if he could catch any whispers or snickers. Even when he did, he didn't say anything. He just scowled.

Mr Cooper, Jack's form teacher, came into the classroom. He was a huge man. Probably seven feet tall. He was the tallest man Jack had ever seen. OK, he had seen a picture of a man who was nine feet on the internet, but Mr Cooper was definitely the tallest man he'd ever seen in real life. Mr Cooper was probably a bit younger than Jack's dad and he always wore a suit and a shirt, but never a tie. Jack had asked him once why he didn't have to wear a tie like the kids. Mr Cooper told Jack it was because he was a rebel. Jack pointed out that he wanted to be a rebel too. Mr Cooper told him you needed to learn the rules before you could break them. He said Jack was a long way off learning the rules. Jack liked Mr Cooper from that point on. There weren't many people who could stump Jack.

'Settle down, everyone,' said Mr Cooper. 'We've got a special assembly this morning.'

There were groans all over the place.

'Mr Locke wants all the Year Eights in the gym,' Mr Cooper went on. 'He has something he wants to talk to you about.'

There were giggles and 'hooooos' now too.

There was no giggling or hooing from Jack. Instead, his stomach twisted tight and he felt like he needed the toilet. He didn't know how, but he just knew this had something to do with Troll Boy.

# SERIOUS TROUBLE

The head of the school, Locky stood behind a podium in front of the whole of Year Eight and straightened the lapels of his tweed blazer. 'Now, Year Eight,' he said. 'I've called an assembly this morning to discuss an important issue. Bullying.'

Jack's heart stopped.

'And I'm not talking about bullying in school,' said Locky. 'You all know how seriously we take that. What I'm talking about is outside of school. When you all get home and log onto your little computers.'

There were a couple of giggles and snickers around the gym.

'What a loser,' whispered Tyson Schofield, who was in the row in front of Jack.

'I have information to suggest that recently there has been a lot of online bullying or "trolling" as I've been informed it's termed,' said Locky. 'This has to stop. And rest assured, if I find the culprit, they will be in serious trouble.'

# SERIOUS TROUBLE

Jack exchanged a glance with Cora.

Cora shook her head, a worried look on her face.

Tyson put his hand in the air.

Locky drew in a long breath. He coughed a little, clearing his throat. 'Schofield, I hope this is serious?'

'Sir, course it is,' said Tyson. 'Will there be a reward? If we help you catch who it is?'

'Your reward will be helping the world be a better place.'

'Could we have some cash instead?'

Several kids burst out laughing.

Jack wasn't one of them. He was sat there, stiff as a statue.

Locky shook his head. 'Schofield, you never fail to disappoint me. See me for detention after school.'

'But, Sir…'

After a couple of announcements about upcoming trips and events, Locky dismissed everyone. On his way to English, Cora nudged Jack. 'Told you this was a bad idea,' she whispered.

'All right,' said Jack.

'Are you gonna stop now?' asked Cora. 'Before it's too late?'

Jack thought about it. He liked being Troll Boy. It made him feel important, like he finally had something to offer. But he didn't want to get into trouble. His mum and dad would go ape. He'd be grounded for months – *years*, maybe. OK, without Troll Boy, he might have to stew on all the reasons why Chloe knocked him back, and while that would make him miserable, it was better than being grounded for the rest of his life.

'It's gone too far,' whispered Cora.

Jack's stomach groaned and bubbled. He nipped into the toilets. There were a couple of Year Sevens at the urinals. Jack recognised one. It was Mark Jones, Chloe's younger brother.

'All right, Jack,' said Mark, with a smirk on his face.

'All right,' said Jack. He frowned. Mark Jones had never spoken to him in his life. Weird.

Jack wasn't a massive fan of using the toilets at school. He didn't mind going for a pee. But a poo, he wasn't keen on that. If he needed a poo, he always tried his best to save it for when he got home, but there was no saving it today. When you've got to go, you've got to go. And right now, Jack had to go.

He hurried inside a cubicle and locked the door behind him. He dropped his bag on the floor and ripped a few sheets of toilet paper from the roll. He peered down at the toilet. It looked clean enough. But Jack knew germs were so small you couldn't see them. He wiped the seat and dropped the paper in the toilet. He pulled his trousers down and sat. The seat was hard and cold. Nowhere near as comfy as his toilet seat at home. He didn't have much choice though. As he sat there, he looked around the walls of the cubicle and read the messages about Omar Croft being the fittest lad ever. Then something caught his eye. Somebody had written, in marker pen…

## TROLL BOY ROCKS!!!

Jack blinked. He wasn't expecting that. Troll Boy did rock, didn't he? He'd rocked the school so hard, they had to call a special assembly. Maybe the school *did* need someone to put people in their place. To some people, he was a menace. But to others, he was a hero. And sometimes heroes had to do things that put their own necks on the line. Spiderman, Batman, Captain Marvel. They all put themselves in danger to do the right thing. OK, Jack wasn't out there saving the world and kicking bad guys' butts, but he was saying the things everyone wanted to say. So what if he got grounded forever. It was worth it, wasn't it? Isaac Strong had been quiet for days – Troll Boy had taken him down a peg or two. There were other people out there who needed taking down a peg or two as well. Loads of them. Troll Boy could do that. He'd be the peg-taker-downer. Or something! Jack wasn't going to give up on Troll Boy after all. Troll Boy rocked! And as long as there was someone out there who thought he rocked, Troll Boy would be out there doing what he did best.

Being a troll.

# ATTACK OF THE TROLL-LINGS

When Jack got home from school, he kicked off his trainers, dumped his bag in the hall, raced upstairs and powered up his laptop. He looked at the shelf, where he kept all his masks and smiled at the troll.

'We rock,' he whispered.

When he loaded up his page, he was amazed. His video had over ten thousand views and hundreds of comments. And his followers had grown massively too. He had well over a thousand now. From all over the world as well. Jack was buzzing. He felt a sense of power swell inside him. No one had ever been interested in what Jack had to say before. He was glad he'd decided to keep Troll Boy alive.

Jack thought about his next move. It had to be something good. Something to top what he'd done before. Posting insults, that was his bread and butter now. He had to do something more. He could do another video. Then he thought about Cora being the director and he felt a bit miserable. They'd never really fallen out before, but it felt like they might fall out for good if Jack carried on playing Troll Boy.

Then an idea came to him. He could do a competition for all his followers, offering the position of Top Troll to the lucky winner. Whoever trolled Isaac and Chloe best would win. He'd set his army of followers on Chloe and Isaac and sit back and watch!

He typed up a post. Then he stopped. Maybe he should use this new-found popularity to do something positive and useful. He could talk about issues and raise awareness. He could say nice things and encourage his followers to be friendly and say nice things too. He could spread love, not nastiness.

Then he thought about the letter. He thought about how hard it was for him to write it. To send it. Then he thought about how Chloe never even replied. He thought about Isaac and how much he hated him. No one wanted to hear Troll Boy talking about world peace. He wasn't Nice Boy. He was Troll Boy!

Jack typed up a post:

COMPETITION TIME TROLL-LINGS! WHOEVER COMES UP WITH THE BEST DISS 4 ISAAC STRONG AND CHLOE JONES GETS TO BE TOP

# ATTACK OF THE TROLL-LINGS

## TROLL!! DO UR WORSTEST!!!

Jack posted the message on his timeline, satisfied this was his master stroke. It wouldn't even be him who was doing the trolling this time. It would be his troll-lings. He was even pleased with the name he'd created – troll-lings. He was a certified genius. He put his hands behind his head, put his feet up on his desk and breathed out. Ahh. His work here was done.

The next morning, Jack was awake before his alarm even went off, scrolling through his timeline on his smartphone. There were tonnes of comments aimed at Isaac. People were calling him all sorts of horrible and awful things. Jack tried counting the insults, but he lost track after fifty. His troll-lings really had gone to town.

It was the same with Chloe. Actually, no, it was worse. People were calling her fat and lots of other mean stuff. Some people had even tweeted that she should go and kill herself. Jack's mouth watered like he might throw up. Some of the troll-lings had gone *way* too far.

Jack wanted Chloe to feel some of what he'd felt, but he didn't wish this level of abuse on her. Then again, what had he expected? Of course this was what would happen. Each person would want to outdo the last and there was only one way they could do that. By being more and more nasty.

Jack sat in his school uniform, waiting for Cora. It was 8:45 am. Jack sighed. He looked over at his mum, who was drinking tea and reading the morning headlines on her tablet.

'Cora still off sick?' she asked.

Jack thought about telling her the truth, about how he'd fallen out with Cora. Then he realised she'd ask why and that would lead to a tonne of questions Jack didn't want to answer. So instead, he just said, 'Must be.'

There was a knock at the door.

'Maybe she's better?' asked his mum.

Jack jumped up from the sofa. He almost ran through the living room, to the front door.

When Jack opened the door, Cora *was* standing there. She nodded at Jack. 'You ready?'

Jack struggled to keep a big smile off his face. 'I'll just get my bag.' He darted back into the living room, grabbed his backpack, kissed his mum on the cheek and left.

'Hope you're feeling better, Cora,' shouted Jack's mum, as Jack closed the door.

'Erm ... thanks, Jen,' Cora shouted back. She frowned at Jack. 'What's your mum on about?'

'Dunno,' said Jack. 'You know what she's like.'

As soon as they got through the school gates, Jack sensed a buzz about the place. Some Year Seven girls were gossiping and Jack caught the words 'Troll Boy' and 'sooooo funny'.

Cora looked at Jack. She squinted, as though he was examining Jack for something.

'What?' asked Jack.

'Have you been doing your Troll Boy stuff again?' asked Cora.

'Nope,' Jack lied.

Jack couldn't pretend once they got into the classroom though. The other kids were practically humming with excitement.

'Did you hear about last night?' asked David Meredith.

'What about last night?' asked Cora.

'Troll Boy set this competition,' said David Meredith. 'Whoever insulted Isaac and Chloe the worst... or best... I'm not sure. Anyway, whoever won, they got the title of Troll Boy's Top Troll. It was carnage! You've got to check it out!'

Cora shook her head. 'I knew you couldn't give it up,' she whispered to Jack.

'I was going to, but...'

Cora just looked away. She didn't want to hear it.

More kids came in. Tyson and his crew. The girls.

Then Isaac. But no Chloe.

Jack's heart stopped. Oh no. What if something had happened? What if she'd… Jack didn't even want to think about it.

A sheepish Isaac took his seat. He pulled out his strange old book from his bag.

'You got trolled hard!' shouted Tyson. 'The Witch got trolled!'

Everyone laughed.

Jack grimaced. What had he done?

He had to know Chloe was OK. He got out of his seat and hurried over to Isaac's table. Jack glanced at the old book Isaac was reading. He noticed the word 'conjuration'.

'Check it,' said Tyson. 'Love is in the air, every where I look around…'

More laughter from the other kids, but Jack didn't pay any attention. This was way more important than some mickey-taking. 'You OK?' he asked Isaac.

Isaac saw Jack and slammed his book shut. 'What's it to you?'

'I heard about the trolling and that,' said Jack. 'I just wondered…'

'Oh, right, I get it. You have a thing for Chloe. How could I forget?'

'Is she… OK?' asked Jack.

'Not really.'

'She hasn't… you know… hurt herself or anything has she?'

Isaac closed his eyes and shook his head. 'Whoever's doing this – they went too far yesterday. I don't think they realise the damage they've caused.'

'Is she OK though?' asked Jack.

'I hope so,' said Isaac.

Jack swallowed. 'Do you have any idea who it is? This troll?'

Isaac shook his head again. 'I'll find them though. Don't worry. I'm going to track their account. Won't take me long.'

Jack tried to swallow again, but there was nothing for him to swallow this time. 'Well, when you see Chloe, tell her I was… you know… asking.'

Isaac stared at Jack long and hard. He didn't say a word.

Jack slumped in his own seat at the back of the classroom.

Tyson leaned over. 'You and him got a thing?' he asked.

'Yeah, obviously,' said Jack.

'I knew it,' said Tyson, laughing.

'What did you say to him?' asked Cora.

'I was just checking Chloe was OK,' said Jack.

'Why? What's up?'

'Some of the stuff yesterday, it got a bit out of

hand.'

'So what are you gonna do?'

'I'm gonna delete it all,' said Jack. 'Get rid of Troll Boy.'

# THE MESSAGE

It'd gone too far. All of it. He couldn't take back what he'd done, but he could do something about what happened next. As soon as Jack got home, he logged into his account and deleted it. Everything.

Troll Boy would be no more.

The power had gone to his head. He'd become giddy with it. Addicted to the popularity and the notoriety. But it'd gone waaay too far. Enough was enough. He had wanted to upset Chloe and Isaac, but he didn't want to make them ill. He didn't want them to come to any *actual* harm. He just wanted them to feel as dejected and miserable as he'd felt. Now he was sure they felt that. And lots, *lots* worse.

Jack had to face facts. Now Troll Boy was gone, he felt empty. It had been the first time in his life he'd felt like someone. Even though people were only taking notice of him for the wrong reasons.

He stared at the troll mask on his shelf. Yesterday it had filled him with a sense of pride and power. Now, when he looked at it, all he felt was guilt. He didn't want that reminder hanging over him, so he pulled the mask from the mannequin's head and stuck it in the bin.

He turned his Xbox on and picked up his controller. He tried to play *Kings of Dread*, but he couldn't concentrate. It was going to take more than cutting through dastardly demons with chainsaws. He grabbed one of his books from the shelf and tried to read it. But instead he just read the first sentence about ten times and realised it was useless even bothering to try. He tried to write a story, but all he could think about was trolls and that made him feel sick. He'd had enough of trolls.

He couldn't settle at all. He felt restless and anxious. He thought about Chloe and the letter he'd sent and he felt anger and resentment and embarrassment and guilt all over again. It was horrible.

He needed to distract himself, so he went downstairs, pulled on his trainers and told his mum he was going out. Jack grabbed his BMX from the garage and sped down the street. Cora only lived a couple of streets away, so it didn't take Jack very long to get to her house.

Cora didn't have a garage. She kept her bike around the back of her house in a shed. Cora lived with her mum. Her dad lived on the other side of town. She went to stay at his house some weekends and holidays. She liked her dad, but her dad had a new wife and a baby. Cora said she didn't like babies much. All they did was cry and poo.

Jack knocked on Cora's door. After a moment, Cora's mum opened up. She had on leggings and running shoes and a T-shirt that said 'Strong is the new sexy'.

'Hi, Jack,' said Cora's mum.

'Hi Mrs Cole, is Cora there?'

'You can call me Lisa, you know,' said Cora's mum.

Jack gave her a blank look.

'I'm sorry, Cora's out,' she said. 'She said she was calling for David.'

Jack blinked as he thought. The only David Jack knew was David Meredith.

'David Meredith?' he asked.

Cora's mum shrugged. 'Must be. I'll tell her you called.'

'OK,' said Jack. 'See ya.' He turned his bike around and pushed it back along Cora's path. Gutted, he rode his bike home.

His mum wasn't there when he got back in. She'd left a note on the fridge letting Jack know she'd popped to the shops. So Jack didn't even have a parent he could bother. He couldn't ever remember feeling as alone as he did right now. He slumped on the sofa.

Then he got up and trudged upstairs. Turned his laptop on. He wasn't going to create another account. He couldn't.

Could he?

No, he couldn't. Even though he was bored and restless and miserable, he wasn't going to do any more of that. Troll Boy was dead. And it was best he stayed that way forever.

Jack opened his email app. There, at the top of his inbox was an email from someone new.

Someone called 'Troll'.

Jack blinked, rubbed his eyes. He had trolls on the brain. He was seeing trolls everywhere. Trolls trolls trolls. He was sick of flipping trolls!

He looked again, expecting something different, but the sender's name was still Troll.

Jack didn't know what this was, but he didn't like the look of it.

Nervously, he clicked on the email.

TO JACK
I KNO WHO U R AND WHERE U LIVE. IM GOING 2 CUM 4 U SOON. JUST U WAIT. C U SOON :)
TROLL

Jack's heart stopped. This was bad. *Really* bad. Jack was scared. He was terrified in fact. And freaked out.

*Really* freaked out.

He didn't want to see the message any longer. He turned his laptop off by the power button.

It had to be Isaac, didn't it? Isaac had said he was close to tracking Troll Boy down. The email had all Isaac's hallmarks – rubbish spelling and grammar. Jack knew it well. He'd mocked him online about it enough. There was just one thing he didn't know. What did Isaac and Chloe have in store for him?

There was a bang downstairs.

Jack's heart thumped inside him. It was them. They were here for him. He leapt out of his seat. What should he do? All of this Troll Boy stuff was coming back to bite him on the backside. It was going to open its mouth wide and gnash down on his rear end!

Then there was a thud on Jack's floor.

Jack's heart stopped this time.

Then Lloyd, his cat, strolled past Jack's feet. He looked at Jack and tilted his head. It was as though he was wondering what Jack was doing. He sniffed for a moment, then padded away.

Jack was really scared now. His mouth was dry. And this wasn't like the time he tried to talk to Chloe. This was real. This was serious.

But was it? Or was it all in his head? Maybe he'd driven himself mad with it all, thinking about it so much. He'd become obsessed; there was no denying it. Even Cora had said so.

There was another bang downstairs.

Jack closed his eyes and squeezed them tight together. It wasn't in his head. It couldn't be. He wasn't mad. He'd *seen* that email. He could *hear* someone downstairs.

'Jack? You in?' shouted someone.

It took Jack a moment to realise it was his mum. His mum!

Jack raced out of his room and down the stairs as quickly as he could. His mum was in the hallway. Shopping bags were all around her.

'Give me a hand, would you, love?' she asked.

'Course. Yeah.'

Jack's mum paused for a moment. She frowned at Jack. 'Are you OK?' she asked.

Jack nodded.

'You're as pale as a sheet,' said his mum. 'You look like you've seen a ghost.'

Jack thought about the email. It didn't seem supernatural. But maybe it was a ghost? And maybe that's what ghosts did these days? They didn't say 'boo' any more, they sent creepy emails.

# LITTLE JACKY

Jack sat at the dining table waiting for his dad to dish up the Sunday morning fry-up. Jack usually loved Sunday mornings. Him, his mum and his dad would have a lovely cooked breakfast together. It always had the works – sausages, bacon, fried eggs, beans, grilled tomatoes, fried bread – it was awesome. And then, in the afternoon, Jack and his dad would go out to a car boot sale, where his dad would see if he could pick up a few bargains. The Sunday vibes didn't make Jack feel any better today though. All he felt was this sense of dread. He knew something bad was going to happen, he just didn't know what. Or when.

His dad came in holding a couple of plates piled with food. He put one down for Jack and the other for Jack's mum. Jack stared at the eggs and bacon and beans. Normally, it'd make his mouth water. But today, it just made him feel sick. Everything made him feel sick.

His dad came back in with his own plate and sat.

He cocked an eyebrow at Jack. 'Not hungry?' she asked.

'I feel a bit funny,' said Jack. 'Think I've got a bug or something.'

'Well, eat what you want,' said Jack's dad.

Jack's mum came into the room holding her big newspaper in one hand and Jack's troll mask in the other.

Jack gulped.

'I found this in the bin, when I was putting the rubbish out,' she said as she plopped the mucky mask on the dining table.

Jack looked at his mum.

'Jack, you're really pale,' said his dad. 'I think this bug might be serious.'

'What bug?' asked Jack's mum. She sat down and picked up her knife and fork.

'Jack's got a tummy bug,' said his dad.

'Do you want any tablets?' asked his mum.

'I'm OK,' Jack said.

'How d'you reckon your mask got in the bin?' asked his dad.

Jack shrugged. 'Dunno. Lloyd must've got it.'

Jack's dad snickered. 'Kids. You're so weird.'

'Your dad's right, Jack. You are a bit weird,' said his mum. She winked at him.

Jack did his best to smile. 'I get it from you two,'

he said.

'You get it from your dad, you mean!' laughed his mum.

Jack's dad shrugged. 'A bit of weirdness never hurt any one. Unless it's serial killer weirdness, then it probably hurt loads of people. Jack's not serial killer weird though are you, Jack?'

Jack shook his head.

'See, Jen,' said Jack's dad. 'No worries.'

Jack stared at the mask on the table. It was like a sign. A bad omen. Jack pushed his plate away.

Later that day, Jack didn't go to the car boot sale with his dad. In fact, he didn't do much at all apart from lie on his bed, stare at the ceiling and worry about what was coming next.

'Oi!' said someone.

Jack blinked. There was only him in there, unless Lloyd had somehow developed the ability to speak, so he had no idea who was talking.

'Oi! Snotball, over 'ere.'

Jack looked down to the bottom of his bed.

He gasped.

His heart stopped.

There was a creature sitting there.

Jack pulled himself back against his headboard. Was he seeing things? Had all this stuff sent him cuckoo? Was it something his over-worked brain had imagined? Stress did funny things to people. His mum had had two months off work last year because of it. And Jack *was* stressed. If he was seeing things, it was probably understandable – under the circumstances.

The creature grinned at Jack as it picked its nose.

Jack scrunched his feet closer to himself and further away from whatever *it* was.

The creature dug a slimy snot ball out of its nose. It stuck it in its mouth and licked its lips.

It was a horrible little thing, about the size of a newborn baby. Its face was all twisted up and it had a massive mouth. It was a brownish green colour like a toad. It had on these white pants too, like the Y fronts Jack's dad wore. They were way too big for it though. It had to hold the pants up so they didn't fall down.

'What…what are you?' asked Jack. 'What do you want?'

'I is Troll,' said Troll. 'And Troll is here to make your lifesies a miseries.' He grinned at Jack with his massive mouth.

Jack didn't know what he should do. Call for his mum? Hide under his bed?

'Have I gone mad?' asked Jack.

Troll shrugged. 'Little Jacky doesn't look very wellsies to meesies.'

Jack looked around the room. Then he saw his

baseball bat. Without thinking, he jumped off his bed. Grabbed the bat.

'Get out of my house!' shouted Jack. He swung his bat at the troll.

But the bat didn't smash the creature in its twisted face as Jack imagined it would. It just went through him. The creature was immaterial. Like a ghost or something.

Troll grinned. 'No point messin' on with that,' he said. 'Little Jacky can see Troll. But Little Jacky cannot hurt Troll, see.' Troll picked his nose again. This time though, instead of eating his snot, he flicked it at Jack.

Jack swatted Troll's snot away. The thought of being splattered with troll snot was horrible.

'What are you?' asked Jack. 'Are you a ghost?'

Troll laughed. 'I'm Troll, Little Jacky. I did tells Little Jacky this.'

'Are you going to eat me or something?' asked Jack. He didn't care if the bat did go right through Troll. His grip around the weapon tightened.

'Hmm…' Troll rubbed his little green chin. 'Maybe I mightsies. Before that though, Little Jacky is goin' to make Troll strong.' He rubbed his little pot belly like someone who'd just eaten a huge meal.

'What you on about?' asked Jack.

'Just wait and seesies,' said Troll.

There was a knock at Jack's door. Jack's heart leapt

again. It was a good thing Jack was only twelve. If he'd had been his gran's age, he'd have probably had a heart attack by now.

The door opened and Jack's mum stuck her head in. 'Did you call me?' she asked.

Jack shook his head.

Her eyes flicked to the baseball bat in Jack's hand. She frowned. 'What're you doing with that?'

Jack frowned too. He looked at his mum, then over at Troll.

Troll smiled at him. It was a creepy, slimy smile.

'Do you not see it?' Jack asked.

'See what?' asked his mum.

Jack pointed at the troll on the end of his bed. 'That? Do you not see that thing there?'

'What thing where?' she asked. 'What is it I'm supposed to see?'

Jack stared at the thing. Only he could see it? It had to be in his head, didn't it? He thought for a second, about telling her there was a baby-sized Troll standing on the end of his bed. Wearing Y fronts. But she wouldn't believe him. They'd take him to doctors who'd ask him weird questions. If he wasn't mad already, by the time all the doctors had finished with him, he would be.

'It's a… it's a spider,' said Jack.

'A spider?' said his mum. 'A baseball bat's a bit over

the top for a spider, isn't it?'

'It was a big one,' said Jack.

'I guess it must've been.' His mum came over to Jack. She brushed his hair from his forehead and pressed her fingers against his head. 'You do have a temperature,' she said. 'Do you want anything?'

What Jack wanted was for Troll to disappear to wherever he'd come from. What Jack wanted was to go back in time and never send any of those horrible messages. What Jack wanted was to wish away the horrible mess he was in. But his mum couldn't do anything like that. She could make him a cup of tea and a sandwich. She could tell him everything was going to be OK. None of that stuff was much use to Jack right now, so he shook his head. 'I'm OK,' he lied.

'Well, if you want anything, just shout,' she said. She kissed him on the head and went to the door. 'And next time, just put it in a glass and take it outside. It hasn't done anything to you. Even if it is a big one.' She smiled at him and left the room, closing the door behind her.

Jack looked at the troll on his bed. 'How come… how did she not see you?'

'Only Little Jacky can see Troll,' said Troll.

'Stop calling me Little Jacky!' said Jack.

'Rights you is… Little Jacky,' Troll grinned again.

# CONJURATION

Jack stared at himself in the bathroom mirror. It had to be in his head. What other explanation was there for it? His mum was right. He was pale. He looked tired too. He hadn't really been sleeping, so it was hardly surprising.

Behind him, he could see Troll sitting on the toilet, in his oversized pants, with that horrible grin on his face.

'Little Jacky is right to wash,' said Troll. 'Little Jacky's a bit of a stinky stonk!'

'Get lost!' said Jack. He ran the tap and splashed water over his face.

Jack stared into the mirror again.

Troll was still there – that horrible, stupid smile still on his face.

Jack lay down on his bed and closed his eyes. The best thing he could do now was sleep. Maybe, when he woke up, Troll would be gone and his brain would be back to normal. It might be like restarting his computer when it crashed.

He rolled onto his side.

'Stinky stonk, stinky stonk,' sang Troll. 'Little Jacky is a stink stonk.'

Jack groaned. He grabbed a pillow and pulled it over his head.

'Don't suffocates, Little Jacky,' said Troll. 'There's is plenty more fun to have yet!'

Jack yanked the pillow off his head. He looked around the room for Troll.

Troll was in the corner, picking his nose.

Jack hurled his pillow at the little creep. But it passed right through Troll and smacked the wall.

Troll laughed. 'Is Troll gettin' you mad, Little Jacky?'

'Just shut up!' said Jack.

'Troll thinks Troll is gettin' Little Jacky all mad!'

Jack sat up in his bed and opened the drawer of his bedside table. He grabbed some earphones, stuck the plug into his phone and flopped back onto his bed, with the earphones in his ears. He pressed play on his music app. He could still hear Troll singing though. So he turned the music up louder until he couldn't hear Troll at all. No singing. No nasty names. No annoying voice. Nothing at all.

He opened an eye.

Troll was standing over him, staring at him. 'Boo!'

said Troll.

Jack jumped. He swiped at Troll, but his hand just passed right through the little monster.

Troll laughed.

Jack buried his face in the pillow. He thought he liked being scared. But the difference was he could always turn off a movie or a game if things got too much. He couldn't turn this off. Whatever *this* was.

Jack opened his eyes, pulled his earphones out. His clock told him it was just after seven in the morning.

Then it all tumbled and toppled into his head.

The nasty little troll.

He looked around his room. Troll wasn't on the foot of his bed, or in the corner of his room. Jack breathed a bit easier. Maybe Jack's brain had sorted itself out after some sleep? Whatever happened yesterday was only a temporary malfunction. A blip.

'Morning, Little Jacky.'

Jack's head swivelled.

There he was. The horrible little thing was up on the shelf where Jack kept his masks. Jack's heart sank. Whatever was happening to Jack, a night's sleep wasn't going to sort it.

'Little Jacky does not look well,' said Troll. 'Little Jacky is lookin' green around them gills.'

'Get stuffed,' said Jack. Jack climbed out of his bed. He pulled on his slippers and dressing gown, and trudged downstairs. He found his mum in the kitchen. She wasn't alone either.

Troll was up on the work surface picking his nose.

Jack shot an angry look at the horrible little thing.

'Morning, baby,' said Jack's mum.

'Mum, I still don't feel well,' said Jack. 'Don't think I should go to school today.'

His mum squinted at him, like she always did when she was checking to see if he was faking. He wasn't though and she knew it.

'OK,' she said. 'You haven't been right these last few days. Will I make you an appointment with the doctor?'

Jack shook his head. 'No, not yet. I'll see how I feel later.'

'Probably best to see the doctor, Jack. I know you don't like it. But if you're not well, you should go.'

'I will,' said Jack. 'If I still don't feel well tomorrow. I'll go then. OK?'

'OK,' said his mum. 'I'll call school. Do you want me to ring Cora's mum or will you text her?'

'I'll text her,' said Jack.

'Your dad'll be home all day,' she said. 'I'll tell him to keep an eye on you.'

Jack smiled at her sadly. It was a weight off. School sucked enough as it was, Jack couldn't imagine how bad it would be with an imaginary troll in tow.

He trudged back upstairs, grabbed his phone and thought about texting Cora. But what was the point? She'd probably just be calling for David Meredith anyway.

In the bathroom, Jack turned on the shower. He put his hand under the water and waited as it heated up.

'You gonna watch me shower?' Jack asked Troll.

Troll nodded then grinned.

'Don't you think that's a bit creepy?' asked Jack.

Troll nodded and grinned again.

'I hate you,' said Jack.

'Troll hates Little Jacky too,' said Troll.

Jack snarled. He checked the water with his hand. It was warm enough. He pulled off his dressing gown and kicked off his slippers. Then he climbed into the shower without taking his boxers off.

'Makes sure Little Jacky washes his stinky bum!' said Troll.

Jack dressed, putting clean boxers on underneath a big bath towel. Troll followed his every step. He was like a horrible, ugly, baby-sized shadow.

'Do you have to keep watching me, you creep?' asked Jack.

'Does it makes Little Jacky angry?' asked Troll.

Jack swallowed. He didn't say anything, but he was pretty sure Troll would be able to tell he was angry.

Troll shrugged. 'It makes Little Jacky angry, it makes Troll happy!'

There was no getting away from it. Jack's day was going to go badly. How could it not? This was probably the first in a long line of extra-sucky days.

A miserable Jack powered up his laptop and typed a question into Google: 'How do I know if I'm mad?'

There wasn't anything in the article about seeing trolls, but there was lots about sleeplessness, paranoia and irritability. This wasn't good. Jack had experienced all of those things lately, hadn't he?

Jack was totally miserable.

Lloyd leapt onto his lap.

Jack stroked the cat. 'You still love me, don't you, Lloydy?'

'Troll likes Little Jacky's slippers,' said Troll.

Jack looked down at his feet.

Troll was there, stroking Jack's Bigfoot slippers.

Jack tried to kick Troll away, but his foot just went through the little creature.

Troll laughed.

Lloyd leapt from Jack's lap.

'Hey, boy, it's OK,' said Jack. 'It's OK.'

Troll screwed his face up, all disgusted. 'Cats is nasty 'orrible beasties,' said Troll. He scrambled away under Jack's bed.

Lloyd scampered out of the room and a thought

came into Jack's head. Maybe he sensed Troll too? Jack remembered reading somewhere that animals could sense the supernatural sometimes.

He thought about Isaac and Chloe. The Witches of Wolfchester. He remembered something. The day when Chloe hadn't gone to school, when Jack had gone over to Isaac and sat next to him, he'd seen something in that old book Isaac always had with him.

'Conjuration.'

Jack did another search. This time for 'conjuration'. The search pulled up loads of stuff about computer games, which was of no interest to Jack. Not today anyway.

What Jack was really after was what the word meant. The word had a few meanings. They went like this:

1. *The act or art of conjuring.*
2. *A magic spell or incantation.*
3. *A magic trick or magical effect.*

Maybe this explained everything? Maybe Isaac and Chloe had somehow pulled off a magic trick. Jack didn't know how exactly that would've worked, but what he did know was that Isaac had an old book that said 'conjuration' in it. Maybe Isaac and Chloe were

called The Witches of Wolfchester for good reason.
Maybe they could do all that hocus-pocus after all?

Jack took a breath. This was crazy. But it did sort
of make some sense. Sort of. If Isaac and Chloe had
performed some sort of magical trick on him, he
could cancel it out, couldn't he?

Jack wasn't sure. What he did know was that he
needed help with this. He pulled his phone out and
scrolled through his address book until he came to
Cora. He called his friend.

After a moment, Cora answered.

'What are you doing?' asked Jack.

'I'm at school,' said Cora. 'What do you think I'm
doing?'

Jack remembered how annoyed he was Cora
might've been hanging out with David Meredith.
'Who's there?' asked Jack.

'What do you mean?' asked Cora.

'Is David Meredith there?'

'Erm, yeah. Why?'

'Look, Cor, I need your help. I need you to come
over.'

'What? Now?'

'Yes now!'

'I can't,' said Cora. 'I'm *at* school.'

'This is important. *Really* important.'

# A GROWING PROBLEM

Jack sat on the sofa, rocking back and forth like he needed the toilet. He didn't need the toilet though. What he needed was a friend. Someone he could talk to about all of this craziness. If he didn't talk about it, he felt like his head might pop.

There was a knock at the door. Jack leapt out of his seat and ran to answer it.

Cora was there.

'Come in, come in,' said Jack. He knew his dad wouldn't bother them, because he'd heard him shouting at a game he was "testing" downstairs.

'What's up?' asked Cora. 'And make it quick. I need to get back before break's over.'

'That's the thing, Cor,' said Jack. 'I don't know.'

Cora frowned. 'How'd you mean?'

'Look, what I'm about to tell you, it's proper mad.' Jack virtually dragged Cora into the living room. They both sat on the sofa. In the corner of his eye, Jack caught a glimpse of Troll. He was perched on the

TV. And surprise surprise he was picking his nose.

'You'll poke your brains out one of these days,' said Jack.

'You what?' asked Cora.

'Nothing. Sorry. Let me explain,' said Jack. 'Isaac knows. He knows about Troll Boy.'

'How do you know?'

Jack thought about it. 'I deleted everything. All of my accounts, like you said I should. I even chucked my troll mask out.'

'You loved that mask,' said Cora.

'I know. It was my favourite. But I couldn't stand to look at it. I felt so rubbish about what I'd done. I just wanted to forget it all.'

'OK.'

'Then I got this email,' said Jack. 'It was really weird and it said it was from Troll. That was it. Just "Troll."'

Cora frowned.

Jack looked over at Troll.

Troll smirked.

'I think Isaac and Chloe did something to me.'

'What d'you mean? "Did something"?'

'She won't believe you,' said Troll.

'I don't know exactly what,' said Jack.

'She'll think you're all fruity and loopy,' said Troll.

'There's a troll in my house,' said Jack.

'A what?'

'There's a troll in my house,' Jack repeated, except now he felt sort of silly when he said it out loud.

'Is this another one of your wind-ups?'

'You've gotta believe me. I think Isaac and Chloe put some sort of spell on me.'

Cora frowned. 'A troll?'

'Yeah.'

'Like an *actual* troll?'

'Well it's more like a ghost troll, if anything.'

'A ghost troll? Is that even a thing?'

'I know it sounds nuts.'

Troll grinned and nodded, while he poked his finger up his left nostril. 'Sure does sound nutsies,' he smirked.

'I know what you're thinking,' said Jack. 'But you've gotta believe me.'

'So where is it then? This ghost troll?'

'I'm right heresies,' said Troll. He stuffed the big blob of snot on his finger into his mouth.

Jack's face twisted in disgust. 'This is the thing – only I can see it.'

'Only you can see it?' repeated Cora.

'And Lloyd. He saw it too. Maybe. Possibly. I don't even know. But no one else. It's in this room right now.'

Cora's eyes flitted around the room. 'Where?'

# A GROWING PROBLEM

'It's OK, you can't see it,' said Jack. 'It can't hurt you or anything.'

'So where is it?'

'It's on the TV.'

Cora blinked. 'Riiight.'

'I swear it. It's the size of a baby. And it wears pants too – Y fronts.'

'A ghost troll in Y-fronts?' she asked.

When she said it out loud, it didn't just sound silly – it sounded ridiculous. 'Yeah,' said Jack, all sheepish.

'I don't get it, Jack. It's a joke, right? Are you filming me or something?' She looked around again, this time for a camera.

'Told you, Little Jacky,' said Troll. 'Even your bestie won't listen.'

'No, I'm being serious. There really is a baby-sized troll sitting on the TV, that only I can see.'

Cora stood up and walked over to the TV. Then she peered down the back of it to where all the tangled wires were.

Jack watched as she passed through Troll.

Troll giggled sickeningly. 'That ticklesies.'

'There's nothing here,' said Cora.

'I've told you, only I can see it.'

'I think you need some help,' said Cora.

'I do,' said Jack. 'That's why I called you. I need to get something – a book.'

'What book?'

'Isaac's magic book.'

'I think you need some *professional* help. Like a doctor or something.'

Jack jumped up from the sofa and marched over to Cora. He grabbed his friend's arm. 'They've done something to me. I'm telling you.'

'You're hurting me, Jack,' said Cora.

Jack realised he *was* hurting his friend and let go of her arm. 'I'm sorry, I didn't mean...'

'I don't know what you're up to. But you can leave me out of it this time.' Cora stared directly at Jack. 'You're right, there *is* a troll in this room. I wish you'd never started all this!' She hurried towards the living room door.

'Wait, Cor, please don't go,' said Jack.

Cora stopped at the door. 'Dave was right about you,' she said.

'David Meredith?' asked Jack.

'Yeah.'

'Right about what?'

'He said you didn't have any respect for me,' said Cora. 'He said you didn't realise how lucky you were to have a good friend like me. And he was right.'

'Well, why don't you go and *marry* him then!' said Jack.

Cora glared at Jack one last time, then marched

out of the room. The front door slammed.

Jack cringed at the sound.

'That went well, Little Jacky,' said Troll.

That was it. Enough was enough. Jack was angry now. Steaming mad. Cora was the only person who would even think about taking Jack seriously. And now she was gone. Jack couldn't take it any more. He snapped.

He lunged at Troll. Tried to grab him, to knock him off the top of the TV, but his hand just passed through the creature. Of course it did. Jack screamed.

'Good,' said Troll. 'Troll likes when Little Jacky gets mad.'

Then something happened. Something scary and weird and freaky.

Troll started to grow right in front of Jack's eyes. He twisted and juddered as his arms stretched and his legs thickened. As scary as it was, it was a pretty amazing sight too. It was like watching something from a horror movie with amazing grotesque special effects. Troll rolled his head slowly around on his neck. Then he interlocked his fingers, turned his hands out and pushed them out as though he'd just finished a work out.

'Ooh,' said Troll. 'That's is muuuch better.'

Troll had pretty much doubled in size. He was as big as a toddler now.

Jack was scared. What was he going to do? What if Troll kept growing and growing, until he was the size of Godzilla?

He had to get away. He raced up the stairs and into his room. He slammed the door shut. Then he pushed his bed against the door, forming a barricade.

He took a step back and listened out for Troll's insulting songs. There was nothing. Silence.

Maybe he'd gone? Maybe he'd got what he needed – he'd ruined Jack's friendship and he'd grown into a small, child-sized troll. Maybe that's all he wanted?

'Psst. Little Jacky!' said Troll.

Jack spun around. Troll was standing on his desk, with his hands behind his back.

'What's Little Jacky doin'?' asked Troll.

'Just leave me alone!' shouted Jack. He dragged the bed out of the way and ran down the stairs. He pulled his trainers on and raced out of the house. Jack ran and ran. He had no idea where he was going. All he knew was that he had to get as far away from Troll as he could.

'Little Jacky!' he heard Troll shout.

Jack looked back. Troll was waddling down the street after him, holding up his huge pants. He moved like a toddler with a full nappy.

'Leave me alone!' shouted Jack.

'Never!' shouted Troll gleefully. 'Never ever!'

# A GROWING PROBLEM

Jack ran down his street and onto Pike Lane. He paused for a moment to see whether he'd shaken the annoying little troll off his trail.

Troll leapt up onto the roof of a car. 'I sees Little Jacky!' shouted Troll. 'Troll likes to play some hides and seeksies!'

Jack turned and ran. He carried on along the lane and around the corner. Then he was at the shopping precinct. There were all types of shops. A pet shop, a supermarket, a hardware store.

Jack knew Troll was still behind him, waddling after him. He could hear him singing his horrible songs.

An old lady shuffled past Jack, dragging a tartan patterned shopping trolley behind her.

Troll appeared on the trolley. 'Mornin', Little Jacky!' said Troll.

Jack squeezed his eyes shut. He curled his fists into balls and ran on. He darted into a shop that sold birthday cards and toys.

'Is Little Jacky tryin' to avoid me?' asked Troll. Troll was up on a shelf next to a huge stuffed teddy bear. He put his arms around the toy as though they were buddies.

'I'll get rid of you,' said Jack. 'Just watch me. I'll send you back to whatever place it is you come from.'

'Ooh,' said Troll. 'Troll is scared.' He laughed.

'Troll has told Little Jacky. Troll is with Little Jacky for ever and ever.'

'I hate you! Why don't you just get lost!' snapped Jack.

'I beg your pardon,' said the shop assistant behind the counter.

'I'm sorry, I err...'

'Don't bother making excuses,' interrupted the woman. 'You youngsters are so rude these days. You think you can say anything you like!'

'I don't, honestly,' pleaded Jack.

'Well I'm pig sick of it,' said the woman.

'Pig sick,' repeated Troll. He rubbed his belly. 'Hmm, Troll feeling hungries.'

'Out. *Now*,' demanded the woman.

Jack didn't know who he was more scared of, Troll or this woman. He raced out of the shop and into the precinct. He looked around. It didn't matter where he went, he wouldn't be able to shake Troll from his tail. Not without that book. He had to get that book from Isaac.

# BAD TO WORSE

Jack trudged home.

Troll waddled along beside him.

Jack looked down at the little creature every now and then.

Troll looked up at Jack and grinned every now and then too.

'This is nicesies, ain't it, Little Jacky?' asked Troll. 'Troll likes to takes a little stroll every once in a while. Lovely day for it, ain't it?'

Jack didn't say anything. It was a lovely day. There was no denying it. The sun was beating down and the people they passed on the street all seemed so happy. That's what the sun did, aside from sending dogs and Year Tens mad, it put smiles on people's faces. Well most people. Jack didn't imagine there was much right now that would put a smile on his face. He was as miserable as he could ever remember.

'What does it feels like, Little Jacky, to not have any friendsies?' asked Troll.

'Shut up,' said Jack.

'Troll thinks yous is gonna end up all crusty and old and covered in wee. A right old stinky stonk!'

Rage ripped through Jack all over again. 'LEAVE ME ALONE!' he screamed.

'Good, Little Jacky!' said Troll. 'That's it!'

Troll started to grow all over again. He twisted and contorted and juddered and stretched. When he was done, he was the size of a six year old – half as tall as Jack.

'Troll hates Little Jacky,' said Troll. 'But Little Jacky does give Troll a nice good feeding!'

When Jack walked in, his dad was waiting for him, a face full of worry. 'Where have you been,' he asked.

'I needed some fresh air,' Jack told him.

'You should've said, I'd have come with you.'

'It's fine Dad,' said Jack. 'Just leave it.'

Jack moped upstairs.

And that evening, Jack moped about his house. There was no point going anywhere else, Troll was with him all the time. There was no getting away from the little creature. Jack had his earphones in, his music up on full. OK, he might have to look at the horrible little troll, but he didn't have to listen to him.

Jack sat at the kitchen table for his tea. His mum was already there, reading one of her social work books. 'Still not feeling well?' she asked.

Jack shook his head.

Jack's dad appeared with two plates of food. He put one each in front of Jack and his mum. 'I've only done you a bit, son,' he said. 'I know you're still not right.'

'I think we need to get him into the doctors tomorrow,' said Jack's mum.

Jack shook his head. What was the point? He'd have to lie to the doctor wouldn't he? He couldn't very well say that someone had cast a horrible magic spell on him.

'It's OK,' said Jack. 'I feel a bit better. I'm going to go back to school tomorrow.'

Jack's mum and dad exchanged a look.

'You sure?' asked his mum.

Jack shrugged. 'It'll probably make me feel better, doing something.'

'OK, well if that's what you want,' said his dad.

It really wasn't what he wanted. Jack had no idea what it would be like going to school with Troll. But he had no choice. He had to confront Isaac and Chloe and demand they undid whatever curse they'd put him under.

Jack stared at his food. Pork chops and potatoes and vegetables. It was one of Jack's favourite meals, but he didn't have much of an appetite.

'Jack?' asked Jack's dad. 'Is there anything going

on? You know, at school or anything?'

Jack shook his head. 'Like what?'

'Is anyone giving you any grief?'

Jack looked across the room. Up on the wall unit where Jack's dad kept all his fancy glasses and cutlery, Troll was there, scratching his bum. He winked at Jack.

Jack thought about the question. Maybe he should tell his parents what was happening. OK, he'd have to explain the letter and the Troll Boy accounts and he'd be in trouble, but he was already in trouble wasn't he? Trouble didn't get much worse than being stalked by a creepy little troll. His parents would protect him, wouldn't they? They loved him. They wouldn't let anything bad happen to him.

Jack nodded. He was going to tell his mum and dad everything. At the very least, he might feel less miserable. 'Actually,' said Jack. 'I do have a problem.'

Jack's dad looked at Jack's mum. 'You can tell us anything.'

'You know that,' said Jack's mum.

'No, you can't,' said Troll. 'You can't tell anyone anything. Peoples will think you're crazy – cuckoo in a clock.' And then he started to make this noise. 'Cuckoo. CUCKOO. CUCKOOOO.'

'Would you just leave me alone?' snapped Jack.

'Erm, we're just trying to help,' said Jack's dad.

'No they're not,' said Troll. 'No one wants to help Little Jacky. Everyone's laughing at him behind his back. Laughings and laughings and laughings...'

'JUST STOP!' screamed Jack at the troll.

Jack pushed his chair back and stood up straight. 'I'm sorry,' he said.

Jack hurried out of the room and up the stairs. He slammed his bedroom door behind him. His *Dr Who* poster slid down the wall. Jack stomped over to the window and pushed it open. He stuck his head into the warm summer air and screamed.

*ARGHHH!*

He took a few breaths to calm himself. Then he screamed again.

*ARGHHHHHH!*

When he turned around, Troll was standing there in front of him, the same height as Jack now. He grinned at Jack.

'Little Troll not so little any more, is he, Little Jacky?'

The next day, Jack got up and got ready. He didn't say anything to his mum and dad. He didn't bother waiting around for Cora either. What was the point? He just grabbed his school bag and left.

'Where's we goin', Little Jacky?' asked Troll, when they were halfway along Jack's street.

'School.'

'Ooh, that sounds like funsies.'

A shiver rolled along Jack's back. He had no idea what trouble Troll would cause for him. He thought about turning around, heading home and telling his parents he didn't feel well enough for school any more. There was no point though. Not now. Not after last night. They wouldn't listen. They'd think he was just pulling some dumb stunt. So he trudged on and braced himself for whatever it was that was coming his way.

Maybe he deserved all this. What he'd done had gone too far. He was in no doubt about that. Maybe he should just take it on the chin. Put up with Troll. The thought made him feel a little better, somehow, but not much.

Cora was already in class, sitting next to David Meredith. They were both huddled over some video game magazine. Cora looked up at Jack. Then she looked away as though Jack didn't even exist.

Jack sat at the back of the classroom.

Troll sat on the seat next to him. He grinned at Jack.

Jack blinked. Then he smirked and shook his head. As horrible as this all was, he had to laugh. Here he was, at school, and sitting next to him was a Jack-sized troll in Y fronts. If Jack had seen that online or on TV, he'd have laughed.

'What's is funny, Little Jacky?' asked Troll.

Jack snickered, but he didn't say anything. Nope. He wasn't going to speak a word to Troll. Not when there were other people around. People probably thought he was weird enough as it was, he didn't want to be known as The Boy Who Talked to Himself.

Chloe and Isaac came into the classroom. They both stared at Jack as they headed for their seats. Chloe looked paler than normal, like she was sick. Jack thought about all the trouble he'd caused her and he felt terrible. Maybe he really did deserve his Troll Curse.

But he'd learned his lesson, hadn't he? He'd suffered too. He was convinced they were responsible for Troll and he was going to confront them. As soon as he had the chance and they were alone, at break or lunch, he was going to have it out with them. Jack craned his neck and tried to get a glimpse into Isaac's bag, to see if he had that weird old book with him. He couldn't see it. He had it somewhere though, Jack was sure of it.

Mr Cooper entered the classroom. 'Morning everyone,' he said. 'Lovely to see you all.'

'Lovely to see you, Sir,' said Tyson.

'Tyson, take that stupid hat off,' said Mr Cooper.

The other kids settled into their seats.

'Look at all these little peoples,' said Troll. 'Think

about how much they hate you Little Jacky. How much they laugh at you behind your backsies. How they all you lots of nasty names...'

Jack stuck his fingers in his ears and tried his best to ignore Troll.

'Weirdo,' said Troll. 'Lame brain. Loser.'

Jack stuck his fingers deeper into his ears, but he could still heart Troll loud and clear. 'LOOSER!' Troll repeated. 'LOOOSER!! LOOOOSER!!!'

'I'M NOT A LOSER!' yelled Jack.

'Jack?' said Mr Cooper.

Jack looked up and realised all the kids in the class were staring at him.

'Are you OK?' asked Mr Cooper.

'Tell him,' said Troll. 'Tell him you're a loser and you're scared you might wet your nicky-nacks. Tell him you're a freaksie, a little weirdy weirdo...'

Jack looked at the faces of his classmates. Cora stared at him, a worried look on her face.

Chloe looked confused. Isaac just smirked.

'They all see it, Little Jacky,' said Troll. 'They all see what an oddity boddity you is.'

'Sorry, Sir,' said Jack. He grabbed his bag and raced out of the room. He didn't stop either, running along the corridor and down the stairs. Through the foyer and out of the school gates.

He had an idea things would go badly, but he

hadn't anticipated it would go so badly *so* soon. It sucked big time having a Troll Curse. He'd been well and truly stitched up by The Witches.

As soon as Jack got home, he kicked off his trainers and dragged himself up to his room. He slumped on his bed and stared at the ceiling.

Troll appeared over him. He bobbed his tongue out at Jack.

Jack rolled over, so he couldn't see Troll any more.

'Have you not had your fun now?' asked Jack.

'Nopesies,' said Troll.

'I've learned my lesson though,' said Jack. 'I've been punished enough, don't you think?'

'Troll likes to gets big!'

'What difference does it make?' asked Jack. 'No one can see you, except me. What does it matter how big you are?'

'Courses it matters'. Troll likes bein' big. Bein' big is funsies! Little Jacky is feedin' Troll good. Troll has to stay. Little Jacky is goin' to make Troll the biggest troll there ever was!'

Jack groaned. What was he going to do?

# CHLOE AND ISAAC

Jack had to do something about Troll. If Troll was around for much longer, he could ruin Jack's life completely. If things carried on the way they were going, Jack could get kicked out of school, which would mean he'd never get a job and he'd end up just like Troll said: lonely and covered in wee. And what about his poor parents? How much would they put up with? They might turf him out too. There really was no telling just how bad this whole mess could get.

There were only two people who could help him: Chloe and Isaac.

Jack waited until just after three. Then he crept downstairs. He stuck his head in the living room. His mum was still at work and his dad was down in his cave, packaging up stuff to send out. Jack pulled his trainers on.

'Where we offsies?' asked Troll. He was sat on the stairs behind Jack, picking his nose.

'None of your business,' said Jack.

'Ooh, a surprise? Troll likes surprisies!'

Jack quietly opened the door and crept out of the house.

He hurried onto Chloe's street and sat on the wall opposite her house. He pulled his phone out and checked it. School was just about finished. Chloe and Isaac would be back soon and when they were, Jack would demand to know what they'd done to him and how to undo it.

Jack clocked Chloe and Isaac at the top of the street. He took a deep breath and marched towards them. This was it. He was going to get to the bottom of this curse. His legs were shaking and his heart was pounding.

'You did this,' said Jack.

'Did what?' asked Isaac. He brushed his hair away from his eyes.

'That book of yours,' said Jack. 'You did a spell or something, didn't you?'

Isaac and Chloe looked at each other.

'I don't know what you mean, Jack,' said Isaac. 'I think you're confused.'

Jack clenched his fists. 'I'm not. I know it was you.'

'Just like we know it was you who pulled all that Troll Boy rubbish,' said Isaac.

Jack relaxed his fists a little.

'Was it you, Jack?' asked Chloe.

Jack stared down at the ground. There was no point pretending it wasn't. He needed to own up for it. 'I'm sorry,' he said.

'But why?' asked Chloe. 'What did we do to you?'

Jack thought about the letter. Didn't she get what she'd done? How could he not have been upset about her blatantly ignoring him? 'You could've just said no.'

Chloe and Isaac looked at one another.

'No to what?' asked Chloe.

'The letter I sent. If you didn't like me, fair enough. But just ignoring me? That was out of order.'

'I really don't know what you're talking about,' said Chloe.

'You know full well I sent you a letter asking you out. Why are you even trying to pretend?'

'I never got any letter,' said Chloe.

'Wait,' said Isaac. 'All that Troll Boy stuff was because you felt rejected?' He looked at Chloe, shaking his head in disbelief.

Jack suddenly felt very embarrassed and very silly. Isaac had a skill for making people feel like that.

'As if you're that immature,' said Isaac.

'What about you two?' said Jack. 'What about what you've done to me?'

'And what have we done to you?' asked Isaac.

'Don't pretend,' said Jack. 'You know exactly what.' Jack pointed over at the wall where he'd been sitting.

Troll kicked his heels against the bricks and waved.

Chloe and Isaac looked at each other all over again.

'We really don't,' said Chloe.

'I've seen your magic book,' said Jack. 'I know.'

'What magic book?' asked Isaac.

'That book,' snapped Jack. 'The one you're always writing in.'

'What's he on about?' asked Chloe.

'Don't ask me,' said Isaac. 'I think he's lost the plot.'

Jack curled his fists into balls. He was getting angry now. If Isaac wasn't going to give him the book, he was going to take it.

Jack lunged at Isaac and swiped at his bag, but Isaac pulled himself and the bag out of the way.

Jack stumbled to the ground. He banged his knees on the concrete path and scraped his hands.

'What do you think you're doing, you weirdo?' snapped Isaac.

Jack picked himself up quickly and spun around. 'Just give it to me,' said Jack.

Isaac pulled himself into some weird fighting pose. His hands were up and he was waggling his fingers like some rubbish magician. 'I do Tae Kwon Do, you know. Don't think I'm afraid to use it.'

Jack wasn't a fighter. He was really angry, but he

wasn't sure he could take Isaac even if Isaac did look ridiculous. He didn't want to fight anyway. He just wanted help. 'Please help me,' he said.

'We really don't know what you mean,' said Chloe.

'Just let me see,' said Jack. 'Let me see your book.'

Isaac shook his head. 'Never help the enemy. That's what my Sensei says.'

Jack narrowed his eyes. He shook his head this time and sighed.

'Does he really say that?' asked Chloe.

Isaac shrugged slightly. 'Sometimes. Depends if he's having a bad day.'

Jack was having a bad day. Actually, he was having a bad few days. It seemed like he was pretty much set for a bad life now too.

'Please,' said Jack desperately.

Isaac stared at Chloe.

'Just show it to him,' said Chloe.

Isaac frowned, before opening his bag. He pulled that old-looking book out. 'This?'

Jack's eyes widened. This was it.

All the answers he needed were inside this book.

# THE CURSE OF JACK

Isaac reluctantly handed the old book to Jack.

Jack grabbed it from him, opened it up. He expected to see all kinds of spells and incantations. But what he found was lots of doodles and verses.

'Is this your spell book?' asked Jack, confused.

'Spell book?' asked Chloe, equally confused.

'It's my journal,' said Isaac. 'We're not *actually* witches.'

Jack stared at the two of them. 'But the troll…'

'I wanted to get you back,' said Isaac. 'Trust me. But Chloe wouldn't let me.'

'She… you didn't do a spell on me?'

'What are you talking about, Jack?' asked Chloe. 'What spell?'

Jack stared at Troll, sitting there on the wall, grinning. He didn't understand. 'I saw it though,' he said. 'I saw you writing about conjurations.'

'Were you looking in my book, you nosey pig?' asked Isaac.

'Nosey, nosey piggie,' said Troll.

'Not on purpose,' said Jack.

Troll oinked and snorted like a pig now.

'If you must know,' said Isaac. 'It was a poem.' He snatched the old book back from Jack and flicked through. He turned the book back to Jack and shoved it in his face.

Jack read the words out: 'You're something from my imagination, a dream, a fantasy, a conjuration...' Jack stared at Isaac, confused.

'I wrote it for someone,' said Isaac.

'Who for?' asked Chloe.

'Just someone,' said Isaac, embarrassed.

Jack just blinked. He didn't understand. 'If it wasn't you...'

'If what wasn't us what?' asked Chloe.

Jack didn't know what to say or do now. He just blinked. Was Troll just in his head? He had to be, didn't he?

'I'm sorry,' said Jack, trudging away. 'Sorry for everything.'

'Jack!' shouted Chloe. 'Are you OK?'

Jack didn't answer and he didn't look back.

With every day that passed, Jack became more and more miserable. It was hard not to be miserable with Troll in his ear, constantly mocking and ridiculing him. Troll was as tall as Jack's dad now. A man-sized troll. Troll fed on Jack's reactions and attention, especially Jack's anger. Jack had figured that much. But try as he might, he couldn't *not* get angry with Troll, not with the things he sang and the damage he'd done. Jack hated Troll with a passion and he couldn't ignore the creature. He just couldn't do it, as much as he tried to. He didn't have that kind of strength.

Jack thought about the letter he'd sent Chloe. It seemed so long ago now. As though it was a totally different life. Things seemed so much better back then. OK, he didn't have Chloe. But he had his crush, and hope, and Cora. He'd even had a good relationship with his parents.

What did he have now? Not much, that's what.

There was only one real option Jack could see for himself. He might not be able to rid himself of the ever-growing Troll, but he could rid everyone else of Jack. And they'd all be a lot better off without him. He had to go. He had to remove the Curse of Jack from everyone around him.

Jack waited until after nine, when it was getting dark. He packed some clothes, some toiletries and a couple of horror novels into his school bag. He looked at his collection of figures and masks sadly. He'd miss his things. He'd miss his house. He'd miss his mum and dad. He'd miss Cora. He'd miss Chloe. He'd even miss Isaac Strong.

He emptied his skull money-box of the fifty-three pounds inside and pulled a piece of paper from his drawer. He took a pen out of his pot and wrote only the third letter he'd ever written in his life, after the one to Father Christmas and the one he really wished he hadn't sent to Chloe. It went like this:

Dear Mum and Dad,

I'm really sorry for how I've been lately. I wish I could explain to you what's going on, but I can't and you wouldn't believe me even if I could. I've decided that I'm going to go away from everyone. It's for the best.

I love you both very much. Make sure you cuddle Lloyd lots for me.

I will miss you.

Jack xxx

Tears stung Jack's eyes. 'What's the worst that could happen?' That's what Cora had said when she was trying to convince Jack to ask Chloe out. Well, here was the answer. And it was probably as bad as things could get.

There was a knock at Jack's door.

Jack folded the letter quickly and slid it into his pocket.

The door opened and his dad stuck his head in. 'You OK?' he asked.

Jack held back his tears and nodded.

'You sure?' asked his dad. 'Cuppa? Sandwich? We could even play that *Dread Kings* game if you want?'

'No thanks,' said Jack. 'I'm good.'

'You're positive?'

'Dad,' said Jack. 'I love you.'

'I know mate,' said Jack's dad. 'I love you too.' He smiled at Jack and left, closing the door behind him.

Jack pulled the letter out of his pocket. He unfolded it and laid it out on his desk.

Not long after, Jack crept out of his room and tiptoed down the stairs. He could hear the TV in the living room and his mum talking to his dad about work. He waited there for ten seconds wishing someone would come out and catch him, but they didn't.

He quietly opened the front door and slipped out of the house. At the bottom of his drive, he looked sadly back at what had been his home. Then he turned away and carried on along his street. He took a detour on his way to the bus stop, so he could pass Chloe's house one last time. He looked up at a bedroom window. He didn't even know if it was hers. He wondered what might've been if he'd never sent that letter.

Then he carried on towards the bus stop. Troll walked next to Jack, picking his nose and humming a horrible tune to himself. Jack hated Troll, but what could he do? For whatever reason, he was stuck with the horrible thing.

'Will Little Jacky miss his homesies?' asked Troll.

Jack felt the anger burning in him. He took a breath. Counted to ten. He wouldn't make Troll any bigger. The horrible thing was big enough as it was.

Jack sat down in the bus shelter.

'Will Little Jacky miss his catsies?' asked Troll. 'Troll hates Little Jacky's catsies.'

Jack stared at Troll, then he looked away. All the while, anger grew hotter inside him.

'Will Little Jacky miss his mumsies and dadsies?' asked Troll.

Jack thought about his mum and dad, watching TV in the living room and eating popcorn from a big bowl. He'd sometimes sit in between them when they had a movie night. He felt so sad about never seeing them again.

Troll grinned at him.

'JUST LEAVE ME ALONE!' shouted Jack.

# THE CURSE OF JACK

Troll absorbed Jack's rage and grew all over again. When he stopped growing, he towered over Jack. He must've been seven feet tall. He was as tall as the ceiling of the bus shelter. He was even taller than Mr Cooper.

In the distance, Jack heard the chugging of the bus. He figured he could get a train from the station, once he was in town. He didn't know where he was going. Just away.

'Troll will never leave Little Jacky,' said Troll. 'As long as Little Jacky keeps making Troll bigsies, Troll will be always be here.'

The thought of being tormented by Troll for the rest of his life filled Jack with despair. His life was ruined. He was terrified of what would happen to him. He'd never been anywhere really without his parents, other than on a school trip to France. But that was different, he'd been with other kids and teachers then. Now, he was on his own. *Really* on his own.

Jack stuck his arm out, so the bus would know he wanted to get on.

After a moment, the bus rolled to a standstill near the stop. The doors hissed open.

Jack took one last look behind him, wondering whether this was the last time he'd ever see his home.

Then he climbed on board.

# AN UNLIKELY ALLY

'JACK!' shouted someone.

Jack paused, before deciding the sound was in his head. He was seeing man-sized trolls. Hearing someone shout his name was hardly a big deal.

'JACK!'

He heard it again. It sounded real. This time, he stepped off the bus.

Chloe ran towards him. She was wearing a black hoodie and her butt-kicking boots.

Jack looked up at Troll. There was a scowl on Troll's face. No grin. Just a scowl.

'Are you wanting to get on or not, mate?' asked the bus driver.

'Troll thinks Little Jacky should go,' said Troll. 'He should go away and never come backsies.'

Jack didn't know what to do. But he knew was Chloe was hurrying towards him and he wanted to know why.

'No, it's OK,' Jack told the bus driver. 'Sorry.'

The driver shook his head. 'Flaming kids.' The doors hissed shut and the bus rolled away.

Then Chloe was there, right in front of Jack. He looked at her, up close for the first time. Her eyes were big and brown. They reminded Jack of one of those Japanese cartoon characters.

'I found your letter,' she said. She had it in her hand. The envelope had been torn open. 'My brother took it. Little jerk.'

Jack's heart sank. Cora had been right. She'd never got the letter at all. All of this – everything he'd done – he'd done it for nothing. He felt like such an idiot. Why hadn't he just gone and asked? What a complete and utter loser. But he was a still a little unsure whether this was another trick of his mind. He reached out and took the letter from her. The paper felt cool in his fingers. Chloe was written on the envelope. It seemed real enough. Maybe Chloe was real too. 'What you doing here?' asked Jack.

'Troll thinks it's time we wents,' said Troll. 'Time Little Jacky wents away for good.'

Jack didn't look at Troll and did his best not to listen either.

'I saw you,' said Chloe. 'I watched you pass by my house. I had a bad feeling.'

'Why?'

'Just… you seemed so sad when you came to see me and Isaac,' she went on. 'I've been worried.'

'She *hasn't* been worrieds,' said Troll. 'Little lady is a little liar.'

'Why would you be worried about me?' asked Jack. 'After what I did.'

Chloe sort of smiled. 'Let's go home,' she said.

The pair walked home together.

Then Jack realised something. This was the first time he'd ever been alone with Chloe. A sudden sense of hope filled him. Maybe she didn't hate him. She seemed like she might even care about him a bit. Maybe it was just sympathy, but it was more than he could have asked for.

'I'm sorry,' said Jack. 'About everything. I feel like such a loser.'

'You are,' said Chloe, smiling slightly. 'But your letter was funny. Made me laugh.'

Jack brightened. 'Yeah?' He looked up at Troll.

Troll's scowl was growing. 'She's telling liesies,' said Troll.

'I went way too far,' said Jack.

'Yeah,' said Chloe. 'You *really* did.'

'I hate myself for what I did,' said Jack.

'I believe you,' said Chloe.

'You do?'

'I tried to look at it from your point of view.'

'Yeah?'

'When I was seven, I made a Valentine's card for Sean Williams – this boy in my class. I gave it to him and he showed everyone. I hated him for it.'

'I thought you might've done something like that too.'

'I wouldn't ever do anything like that,' said Chloe. 'I know how horrible it made me feel. Isaac would though. He wanted to.'

'But you didn't let him?'

'Not even after all that stuff you did online.'

Jack's heart sank at the thought. He wished he'd have done things differently. Wished he'd have done everything differently.

'Why do you hang out with him?' asked Jack. 'Isaac. I know I don't really know you, but you... you seem dead nice.'

'He doesn't judge me,' said Chloe. 'Not like the other kids. I can just be myself with him. I don't have to try and fit in.'

Jack understood what Chloe was saying. That was the reason he wanted to hang out with Chloe himself.

'Plus he's got his own stuff going on,' said Chloe. 'There's lots you don't know about Isaac.'

Jack wondered what Chloe meant, but he didn't ask.

'You know, Jack, if I'd have read that letter, before

everything else, I might've said maybe…'

Jack's heart stopped. Then it started pounding so fast, he thought it might burst. 'Really?'

'I might've. Before everything.'

Jack's pounding heart sank even further. It was near his bum now. Not only did he feel like an idiot, he was really annoyed with himself. He'd well and truly messed everything up, hadn't he?

The two of them carried on walking until they were at the bottom of Jack's drive.

'Earlier,' said Chloe. 'You were talking about some troll?'

Jack snatched a sneaky glance at Troll, who seemed to be strangely shorter than before. 'Forget it,' said Jack. 'I was just… my head was all over the place.'

'OK.'

'Stress, I think,' Jack went on.

'Stress?'

'I think I might've got a bit obsessed.'

Chloe didn't say anything.

'I'll be OK though,' said Jack.

'If you ever need to talk,' said Chloe. 'About anything.'

Jack glanced up at Troll, who stood there, smaller, but still towering over him. 'Is there any way I can ever make it up to you?' asked Jack. 'For what I did?'

Maybe,' said Chloe. 'There might be one thing…'

# DON'T FEED THE TROLL

'I better go,' said Chloe. 'My mum will go bananas if she knows I'm out this late.' She handed Jack his letter back.

Jack took it from her. 'Thanks.'

'See you at school, Jack,' she said.

'Yeah, see you at school.' He watched her as she hurried away. For the first time in a long time, Jack felt all right. Not great or amazing or anything, but all right. He took a breath and hurried up his drive. He pulled his key out and slid it quietly into the lock. He turned the key and opened the door.

The living room door opened as soon as Jack closed the front door behind him.

His mum and dad were standing there.

'Jack?' asked his mum. 'Where have you been?'

She didn't let him answer. Instead, she rushed towards him and threw her arms around him so tight it took Jack's breath away.

Jack's dad joined them and they had a group hug right there in the hallway.

After a moment, his mum and dad let him go.

'We found your note,' said Jack's dad. 'Why didn't you tell us how you felt?'

Jack looked up at Troll. 'It… it wasn't that easy.'

'It might not be easy. But you must!' said his mum. 'If ever there's anything's wrong at all, you're not on your own.'

Jack felt even better. Maybe there was hope for him? Maybe, with the help of his parents and maybe even Chloe, maybe Jack could defeat Troll?

The next day, Jack got ready for school, but he didn't go straight there. He took a detour via Isaac's house. Chloe had given him the address and she'd also given Jack a mission. When she'd told Jack what she told him, he was shocked. Actually, he was beyond shocked. He was well and truly gob-smacked.

Troll followed Jack. 'Troll don't see why Little Jacky's doing this,' he said. 'Troll thinks it's a waste of time.'

Jack didn't even look back. He just let Troll's words wash over him. It was starting to get easier to ignore Troll.

He took a breath and strode up the path. But before he could knock the door, someone called his name.

'Jack?'

Jack turned around and saw his mum slamming her car door shut. He frowned, all confused.

'I didn't know you and Isaac were friends,' said Jack's mum.

'We're... erm, not,' said Jack. 'What are you doing here?'

'I work with Isaac,' said Jack's mum.

Jack just stared at her.

'He's one of the kids I work with,' she went on.

'Isaac's in care?' asked Jack.

'He is,' said Jack's mum. 'But I don't think he likes people to know.'

'Right,' said Jack. He thought about what Chloe had told him, about Isaac having his own stuff going on and it all made sense. If Isaac was in care then bad stuff might've happened in his life. Maybe that explained why he wasn't good with people? Jack felt suddenly even more guilty.

'So why are you here?' asked Jack's mum.

'Just some... some school project,' said Jack.

Jack's mum rang the doorbell. After a moment, Isaac answered. As soon as he saw Jack, he scowled.

'Hi Isaac,' said Jack's mum.

'Hi,' said Isaac. He scowled at Jack even harder.

'Troll was rightsies,' said Troll. 'This was a bad idea.'

Jack ignored Troll. 'Hi Isaac,' said Jack.

'Jack was telling me the two of you are working on a school project,' said Jack's mum.

'Yeah,' said Jack, interrupting before Isaac could point out there was no such thing. 'The school project.'

'How do you two know each other?' asked Isaac.

'Jack's my son,' said Jack's mum.

Isaac was frowning as well as scowling now.

'Is Mandy around?' asked Jack's mum.

Isaac opened the door further. 'She's in the kitchen.'

'I'll see you this afternoon,' Jack's mum said to Jack, and she went inside the house.

Jack and Isaac stood there in silence for a full five seconds. It was as awkward as anything.

'What're you doing here?' asked Isaac.

'Chloe asked me to come,' said Jack. 'I didn't know, y'know...'

'What?'

'That you were in care.'

Isaac's expression darkened.

'It's nothing to be ashamed of,' said Jack.

'If you even dare tell anyone...'

'I won't,' said Jack. 'I swear it.'

'You better not.'

'Look,' said Jack. 'I'm really sorry about what I did.'

'I don't care,' said Isaac.

'I know I don't deserve your forgiveness,' said Jack. 'The trouble I caused was way out of order. But maybe I can help you?'

'You?' sneered Isaac. 'How could *you* help me?'

'I could put in a good word,' said Jack. 'With Cora.'

Isaac's pale cheeks went a little bit red. 'What you on about?'

'Chloe told me. That song you wrote. It was about Cora.'

Isaac's face was even redder now. 'No it wasn't.'

'OK,' said Jack. 'Fair enough. I'm sorry, for everything.' Jack smiled sadly and walked back along the path.

Then Isaac called to Jack. 'Jack,' said Isaac. 'D'you... y'know... d'you think she might like me?'

Jack turned back, shrugged. 'Only one way to find out – ask.'

# THE PROM

A couple of weeks later, and it was the end of term prom. Jack's mum and dad had got Jack on the waiting list for a counsellor and Jack hadn't argued. After the misery he'd been through, he thought it couldn't hurt to talk to someone about his problems. In fact, it might even help. Jack knew there were things going on in his head sometimes he didn't understand. He knew too that trying to fix things on his own wasn't the best option.

Jack fastened the top button of his smart shirt.

Troll stood on the bed, watching him. 'Little Jackie looks fat and ugly,' he said. 'He stinks too. A right stinky stonk.'

Jack didn't even react. He just looked at himself in the mirror and smiled. 'Looking good,' he said to himself.

The things Troll said were mean and nasty, but Jack understood they were meant to wind him up and get him angry. They were meant to make him react. The less he reacted, the less effect they had. The less power Troll had over him.

'No,' said Troll. 'Looking bads. Looking really really bads.'

Jack laughed off Troll's comment. Troll was much smaller now. He was baby-sized, just the way he'd been when he first appeared.

'Little Jacky is fat and ugly!' screamed Troll.

'Aww thanks,' said Jack. 'Means a lot coming from you.' He winked at Troll.

Troll – full of anger – jumped up and down on the bed, throwing a total troll tantrum. Jack watched as the creature shrank a little bit more.

There was a knock at the door and Jack's mum and dad came in. Jack's mum put her hand on her chest, bursting with pride. 'Look at you,' she said. 'Don't you look handsome?'

'Yep,' said Jack, winking at Troll.

'Gah!' said Troll, folding his arms and turning away.

'Confident too,' said Jack's dad.

'Take the picture then, Pat,' said Jack's mum.

Jack posed, smiling as his dad took a snap with his camera.

Jack arrived at school. The others were waiting outside the school entrance. Instead of going on dates, they'd decided to all go together. Jack and Cora, Isaac and Chloe, and David Meredith. They'd sort of become a little gang. Cora wore a sparkly red dress. Chloe and Isaac were decked out in black. David Meredith was in some light blue suit that looked like he'd got straight from the sixties.

'You all look amazing,' said Jack.

'Don't look too bad yourself,' said Isaac.

Jack stared at him, pretending to be shocked. 'Did you just say something nice to me?'

'As if,' said Isaac. 'You must be hearing things!'

The five of them went inside.

The school hall was filled with decorations and balloons. Music played and kids from their year were already dancing. Tyson Schofield was body-popping in the middle of the dance-floor, while Mr Cooper and Locky looked on, confused.

'Anyone wanna dance?' asked Cora.

'I will,' said David Meredith.

'Me too,' said Isaac.

Cora held out an arm for each of them and led the two boys to the dance floor.

Jack and Chloe sat, smiling, watching Isaac and David Meredith as they each competed for Cora's attention.

'D'you wanna dance?' Jack asked Chloe.

'Not really the dancing type,' said Chloe.

'Me neither,' said Jack.

'We can just sit and chill, can't we?'

'Yeah, course,' said Jack.

Then Jack realised something. He couldn't see Troll. He scanned the hall, but the little monster was nowhere to be seen.

'You looking for someone?' asked Chloe.

'No,' smiled Jack. 'No one at all.'

# A NOTE FROM JOHN

I really hope you enjoyed reading *Don't Feed the Troll!* How about sharing it with your friends? If you're not already a member of a book club, why not join, or even start one? Book clubs can be great fun, and they give you a chance to talk about all the things you did (or didn't!) like about a book.

Here are a few suggestions of what to think about to get you going. (Of course, you don't have to be in a book club – you can just do it for fun!)

**The book's title...**
- What did you think about this book when you first read the title?
- Did anything about the cover give you a clue as to what the story was really about?
- If you had to rename the book, what would you call it and why?

**The book's characters...**
- How is Isaac made to look like like a bad guy?

- Do you think that Jack was a good friend to Cora? Why/why not?
- How was Troll bad? But how did his appearance help Jack?

**Jack's Troll Boy behaviour was out of character.**
- Why do you think Jack 'trolled' Chloe and Isaac?
- Would it ever be OK to behave the way Jack did? Why/why not?
- What do you think the impact of Jack's actions were on Chloe and Isaac? Jack's parents? Cora? The people who followed Troll Boy?

**Jack had a good relationship with his parents, but he still didn't talk to them about his problems.**
- Why do you think Jack didn't ask his parents for help?
- What advice would you give to a friend who suggested doing what Jack did?
- How might talking about his problems have helped Jack deal with Troll?

**Do you think it was right that things turned out the way they did?**
- What did you think would happen at the end of the story? Were you right?
- Did you feel sorry for Jack? Why/why not?

- Do you think Chloe was right to forgive Jack? Would you have done? Why/why not?

**Would you recommend *Don't Feed the Troll!* to other readers?**
- Were there important lessons to be learned from the story?
- Were there any parts that made you feel uncomfortable? Why do you think that was?
- How do you think the story could be useful in schools?

# DON'T BE MEAN
# BEHIND THE SCREEN!

In the story, Jack feels rejected by Chloe. It's this embarrassment that leads him to become a cyberbully, or 'troll'.

It is all too easy to post a hurtful comment on social media, or in a message. Some people will say things online they would never dream of saying to someone's face, because the anonymity of the internet allows them to feel distant from their victim.

Unfortunately, bullying is something many people will experience at some point in their life: either first-hand as a victim, or as a bystander if someone they know is being bullied. With smartphones and tablets, bullies can harrass their victims day and night, and cyberbullying is having an increasing impact on people's mental health and wellbeing.

However, bullying – whether online or face-to-face – is not something we should have to expect or allow to happen.

There are signs that you can look out for if someone is being bullied. For example, in the story,

Chloe and Isaac become withdrawn and upset as a result of Troll Boy's actions. Here are some helpful websites that offer advice on how to spot, stop and prevent bullying, and how to support anyone who is affected by it.

*www.childline.org.uk/info-advice/bullying-abuse-safety/*
*www.anti-bullyingalliance.org.uk/tools-information/if-youre-being-bullied*
*www.anti-bullyingalliance.org.uk/tools-information/all-about-bullying/online-bullying*
*www.bullying.co.uk/cyberbullying*

## IF YOU ARE BEING BULLIED ONLINE...

1. Don't be tempted to retaliate. That's often exactly what bullies want.
2. Save any evidence you can. Take screenshots and save messages.
3. Tell an adult what's happening.
4. Report it, block the bully, mute the messages.
5. Always remember, the problem is with the bully, not with you.

# ALSO BY JOHN HICKMAN

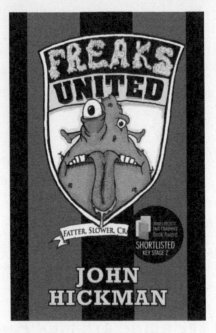

ISBN 978-1-78270-194-1

Seth, Beefy and Angelo can't believe it when they aren't selected for the football team at their new school. And to make things worse, they are labelled the 'freaks' who didn't make it. Do they give up on their dream, or do they find a way to show coach Steele and his squad they're wrong? A fun footballing story about the kids who don't get picked.

*'If you don't know your left foot from your right – and even if you do – Freaks United is a book you'll love. It's great!'* Bali Rai

# FREAKS UNITED ARE BACK!

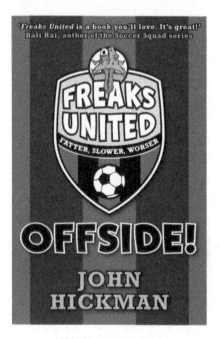

ISBN 978-1-78270-275-7

Seth, Beefy and Angelo and their awkward but determined team of footballing misfits are aiming for glory in their first real tournament. But how do you fit 11 players into a five-a-side team?

Seth makes some dodgy decisions that see him tackling not only the dreaded school coach, Mr Steele, but his friends as well… Can the Freaks' team spirit carry them through, or will Seth's meddling mess up their dreams before they get the chance?

# ABOUT THE AUTHOR

John Hickman is an award-winning writer based in Newcastle upon Tyne.

In addition to his books for children, John has also written for a number of television series, including *EastEnders* for BBC One, and *The Dumping Ground* for CBBC. His children's television script, *The Things*, won the BAFTA Rocliffe New Writing Competition, and his first book, *Freaks United*, was shortlisted for the 2017 James Reckitt Hull Children's Book Award.